Treasured Guest

....

Charlotte Platt

Undertaker Books

Undertaker Books

www.undertakerbooks.com

First edition 2024

EARLY PRAISE FOR TREASURED GUEST

"Treasured Guest is a visceral, immersive, captivating read—echoes of The Shining and Shirley Jackson splashed with Clive Barker's body horror. One of my favorite authors writing today."

-Richard Thomas, author of *Incarnate* and *Spontaneous Human Combustion* (Bram Stoker Award finalist)

"The Basker Hotel in Glasgow prides itself on service, and is always seeking to expand its impressive--and lively--retinue. When former soldier, Stephanie, tries to check out, the Basker offers her a permanent position with them. One it is determined she cannot refuse.

Thankfully, Steph is used to tough situations and is more than prepared to give the Basker a taste, in blood, of exactly how much her life outside its walls is worth to her. Once again, Platt brings her characteristic lush and decadent descriptions to bring the intricacies of the Basker to vivid detail, trapping the audience in with Steph as she fights everything the Hotel throws at her to win her over, or to wear her down--whichever comes first.

Giving us a haunting blend of psychological and visceral, bloody, horror, Steph's despair and frustration at her isolation are as well realised as the disturbing array of tactics the hotel employs to get Steph to reconsider her decision. The juxtaposition of folkloric monstrosities in a hotel--ceiling-height flaming deer-like creatures--and the unfinished stories of the past residents of the room are told with perfect, jump-scare, precision that only add to the well crafted sense of dread.

The Basker is a story that knows how to trap its guests, even after you read the last page, it lingers. Can you really be sure you, the most Treasured Guest, have left it behind?"

-LK Kitney, author of *The Lies We Tell Ourselves*

"Creeping, slow-burn dread at its finest punctuated by satisfying moments of visceral raw violence, Treasured

Guest is a must-read for lovers of claustrophobic hotel horror and cosmic creatures."

-Chloe York, author of *Our Devil's Awake*

"This is the story of Stephanie's journey into The Pit in the strange hotel in Glasgow. This short novel is the work of a true storyteller in the tradition of Dante and Alasdair Gray. The language is both conversational and revelatory as we follow our ever-more traumatised guide into the increasingly sinister and surreal other realm where time, morality and sheer physicality are all turned on their head. There is a dark energetic poetry at work in this narrative which compels both the protagonist and the reader forwards.

Charlotte Platt is a writer with a macabre but compassionate imagination and with all the story's gothic, maze-like horrors and blind alleys, the reader always feel they are in safe hands, because the writer is showing us a chilling dream-portrait of our society now--brutal and often oppressive, yes; and full of blood, body parts and booze--but an important representation of our times none the less. These monsters are terrifying because they are recognisable. Charlotte Platt has gone into the fairy mound on our behalf. The world we live in, however repugnant, as Charlotte Platt makes plain, is our own creation. It is a manifestation of all our baser instincts, selfish fears and long-evaded inner demons. If we want, finally, to change the world, as Stephanie discovers in the story, then we will have no choice but to change ourselves. Treasured Guest is a book everyone should read."

-George Gunn, author of *The Great Edge*, *Chronicles of the First Light*, and more

For Bear, who I am always coming home to.

Treasured Guest

CHAPTER 1

S tephanie hovered at the bottom of the hotel steps, key and bag in hand. It was raining, and she had her umbrella packed for this given all Glasgow had done for the last three days was rain. She didn't fancy getting soaked while she wandered around looking for somewhere to get a good drink.

The chirpy concierge was at the desk again—she presumed he worked night shifts since she hadn't given him her key in the mornings—so she went over to him.

"Thomas, wasn't it?" She waved to catch his attention.

"A pleasure to be remembered." He straightened up, smiling at her. He was in a black shirt and matching trousers today, a little corporate but professional. It made his fake tan a little less sad, at least; understandable he'd want a bit of sun from a bottle if the rain was like this all year.

"I'm looking for a bar. I'm travelling tomorrow so I'm not thinking swinging from the chandelier or anything, but it's been a rough week. Where's good?"

He hummed in thought, glancing out to the pouring weather. "Do you have anything specific in mind? Our bar isn't particularly busy, but Frankie does a mean cocktail and we do have a nice selection of wines."

"You have a bar?" She'd purposefully avoided the mini-fridge in the room lest the usual issue of expenses come up, but a bar was a different matter entirely.

"It's only a wee thing, but it'd save you getting soaked out there again. It's been awful weather this week."

"Yeah I'd rather not swim there."

He laughed at her bad joke and smiled. "Alright, if you go down the same hallway as the lifts and keep going, it's through the sitting room and on your left."

"Thank you very much."

"No trouble." He gave her a firm, if dismissive, nod.

She left him to his computer and went back to the warm little corridor with the lifts, passing the waiting buttons and hunting for the promised bar. The corridor was panelled with dark wood, like the reception area, and the looming dark space of open double doors beckoned ahead.

They led her into a low-ceilinged room with fat, broad armchairs arranged around low tables. Scattered like wildflowers, they sat in little collections here and there, and a fire burned in a stone fireplace she wouldn't have guessed at for toffee. There was no one else in there, so she didn't feel bad for stopping at the fire.

It was banked low, the tail end of what she thought might be logs and peat burning down into quick flickering chunks low in the pit. It smelled like wood smoke, the delicious curl of forest and heat a pleasant surprise. The glow it gave flickered over the ceiling, complimenting the soft light of various tall lamps with tasselled shades, almost like a gentleman's club. It was another something that didn't quite make sense: an open fire and what she'd bet was previously a smoking room tucked away here, an unadvertised bar. It had to be a good day rate, no way the office had just put her here for a laugh.

She drew away from the fireplace, following Thomas's instructions and looking for the doors on her left. They were open too, showing a tall bar with a selection of lit optics leaning forward against their stands. It was as glitzy as the other room, with high red leather stools and mirrors backing the regimented bottles like a 1920s gin joint. Peering in, she checked for signs of life before she stepped over the threshold, spotting a short redhead at the far end.

Coughing to give fair warning, she wandered in, choosing a stool away from the doors. The woman came over to her with a practiced grin, cleaning towel slung over her shoulder.

"Not often I get company this early." Her brows popped as she perched herself on one elbow. She was short as a pixie with a haircut to match, and a smattering of freckles across her face that just invited gazing over them. Trust Stephanie to find the cute bartender the last night she was here.

"Eleven's early?" Stephanie asked, glancing about the empty space.

"Aye, folks are usually out on the lash on a Friday night and come back here once they're tanked up. Don't see much of anyone till gone one." Her accent was all the city, broad as the river, and Stephanie found her own strengthening in response.

"Sorry to disappoint; would you rather I left you to the friendly conversation of the glass washer?"

"Nah, it never listens in an argument," she said, eyes sparkling. "What can I get you?"

"I was thinking a glass of wine, but I'm told your cocktails are impressive."

"Who's been lying to you?" She slapped a hand against her chest in mock surprise.

"Thomas, at the front? I asked him where was good to get a quiet drink and he recommended I come and see you."

"Ah, the dutiful concierge keeping you inside, should've known. I'm Frankie, by the by."

"Stephanie, you can call me Steph. So, do we have a menu to pick from or are you making them on the fly?"

"Well, I can make you any of the usual, or you can let me know some things you like and I can personalise one for you. What's your poison?" She glanced over her shoulder at the selection of bottles.

"Gin or tequila is my go-to, but I don't mind some vodka either. No rum though, too sweet."

"I'll see what I can come up with then. Not too sweet. You'll want something mixed, if you're travelling?"

"Yeah, I get to go home tomorrow. I got sent through for a presentation and to train up a new office. I'm an absolute zombie from it." Stephanie leaned forward, elbows on the bar, opening her phone to text Jenny and see how her Friday had been. She could still be a good girlfriend while having a little flirt with the bartender. Their fight before she travelled hadn't been serious enough to warrant *no* social flirting.

"Sounds tiring. I hate training one new start, never mind an entire office."

"I don't mind the prep, it's mostly the people. Everyone asks the same questions without listening to the presentation I spent forty minutes giving them." She took a quick selfie of her facing away from the bar, so Jenny could see the bottles and maybe also Frankie doing something with a tall glass. "Can I ask you about this place?"

"What about it?" Frankie asked, attention on a dark green bottle of something.

"Has someone bought it recently?"

"Nah. What makes you ask that?"

"The style is a bit mix and match. Like the fire back there, it's a lovely touch, but it's more hunting lodge than city slicker. But your colour schemes on the hallways and the breakfast room are so chic the place looks like it's out of a magazine. It's weird."

"You're spotting the old bits. This place has been around ages; management enjoys keeping the areas with some personality. Makes us seem a bit jigsaw, true, but you'll be hard pressed to find anywhere else like it."

She brought Stephanie a tall glass filled with a layered drink: a cool pink topped with vibrant orange and then a layer of something sparkling.

"What on earth is that then?" Stephanie asked, slipping her phone up to take a photo. This demanded documentation.

"I call this a Doldrums, as in 'down in the'—it's gin and raspberry muddled at the bottom, mango juice and a different gin in the middle, prosecco on top. The best part is the raspberry pieces, so you've got to dig down into them."

"Sounds lethal."

"Only if you have too many, promise." Frankie gave her a wink, moving off to address a beeping machine.

"You been doing this for long?"

"Making cocktails? Longer than I care to admit." Frankie lifted a set of steaming glasses onto the counter, closing the machine lid with her foot. "You been training folk long?"

"Not really. I get sent off for doing it most often. The boss doesn't like sending folk with kids away for work, lest anything happen, and my only babies are my cats so..."

"Interesting approach." Frankie started polishing the glasses, setting them out in neat lines. Her uniform was a little different to Thomas's; she had a white shirt with a black waistcoat tied neatly at her waist. It was cute. And that was the sign Stephanie should not drink more than one of these.

"He just doesn't like the idea of sending anyone's mum or dad off and they die in some horrible accident. Which, you know, is flattering to know I'm expendable, but my cats would probably eat my face if I died in my sleep, so he may have a point there."

Frankie paused, brows rising in consideration. "I suppose a toddler is less likely to do that."

"You hope," Stephanie said, nodding as she snagged the straw and took a large sip. The gin exploded on her tongue, sharp and vicious in the best way, with the smooth sweetness of the mango easing the rest through.

Frankie grinned at her. "It's pretty punchy, made with local gins."

"I'll have to get the brands; this is brilliant. My girlfriend will love it."

"Happy to help." Frankie grabbed an order pad and jotted the names down, tearing it off and folding it neatly in half to give Stephanie. "Now tell me more about these face eating cats."

CHAPTER 2

It had been a while since Stephanie had a hangover that made her teeth fuzzy. She didn't love the sound of her alarm going off, combined with the piercing headache pushing at the edges of her consciousness, and she was going to like it even less when she had to get on a train.

Should have stopped at one Doldrum.

She had vague memories of chatting to Frankie until much later than planned, spilling her guts about Jenny. She couldn't fully remember getting back to her room, but there were bits: leaning back against the handrail in the lifts, walking through corridors that weren't the one she needed. A faint image of the tight stairwells came to mind, the sharp corner turns like those that led to the breakfast room. Had she gone looking for late night breakfast? Please *no*.

She rolled out of bed, silencing her alarm and opening the bottle of water drunk Stephanie had kindly left on the bedside table. She let the water sit in her mouth, warming to blood temperature, before she swallowed—anything too cold was bound to come back up.

Padding into the bathroom, she washed her face and packed her items up as she went, brushing away the layer of sugar in her mouth. The mint toothpaste was overpowering, and she opened her mouth to gag, but nothing else came out.

Wiping her lips and bundling the brush and paste into her shower cap, she went and opened the curtains. It was mostly dark out so it only helped a little, but she carefully scanned for things that needed packing. She had an hour yet, plenty of time, but she was keen to get checked out and have breakfast somewhere else. Preferably at the train station, so she knew she was on the way home and didn't need to plan for what else could go wrong.

Like being an idiot because of a cute bartender.

She set her case out on the bed and bundled everything but her comfortable travel gear and her trainers, which would do her today. She was going to be delicate once the hangover really kicked in so she kept a thin jumper out too. Maybe she wouldn't need it after something decent to eat, but better safe. Sipping a bit more from the water bottle, she tossed that in there too, just in case. A little tub of paracetamol was somewhere in her handbag, if it really tipped into the nasty side.

One last check over the room showed nothing out of place, so she slid her coat on and bundled up; bag on shoulder, case dragged behind her, keys in hand. Checking out would be quick and she had designs on tea and maybe a cheese toasty. Or a croissant. Something with carbs and grease to soak up her shame.

The corridors were silent, and she jabbed the button for the lift while also trying to double-check the train timetables. She should get a notification if there were any delays—the company was meant to email her, or notify her through the app. Those apps were always failing to open properly, though, and her emails were hectic, so she was better checking. She tapped her foot as she waited. Something was off.

Glancing up, she found the floor number display of the lift was blank, no changing red digits to show progress up or down. The neighbouring lift was the same, just a dead screen. Those behind her had their displays flooded crimson, the little digital dots uniformly lit up. Maintenance, maybe, if all of them were out. Clicking her tongue, she stripped her jumper off and went for the stairs—she'd soon heat up lugging her case around.

Each floor had a curving staircase, interrupted part way down by a short middle landing that flanked the lifts but didn't give access, making the stairs feel longer than they should. A quirk of the old building, probably, or a safety measure in case of fire, though the lack of windows or doors made the bright space seem claustrophobic. She was close to the top; the hotel had eight floors, if she remembered correctly. She could stomach carrying her bags down six floors, provided she stopped to sip water when she needed it.

The carpet back here was less plush than those in the corridors, but it changed with the floors—rich teal and moss green flowing into claret red and a creamy stone. The smells of the hotel were more prominent here too, the hot cotton of washing sheets, toasting bread, and brewing coffee.

Her stomach growled and she paused for a moment, pushed against one wall so she didn't block anyone else who may spring up. Puking on the stairs was a special type of messy she didn't want to be, so she rode the sensation out, breathing in through her mouth to minimise the smell.

Her hangover must have been worse than she thought: once she was safe to move again she was going in circles, the same colours and signs accompanying her descent. Here was the blue again, then the green, the identical doors giving her no clue where she was in the building. After passing the blue a further time she ducked into the corridor, seeking a reference point.

A group of women flocked together at one of the "staff only" doors nestled into the far end of a passage, and Stephanie relaxed a little, the bustle of them passing sheets and towels back and forth grounding. She walked towards them, waving a little. A stocky older lady clocked her and stepped away from the others, nodding at them to load up a cart.

"Sorry to bother you. This is probably really stupid but I'm trying to check out and the lifts weren't working, so I was walking downstairs, but I seem to have got turned around at some point. Which floor are we on?"

"Turned around?" the lady repeated, tilting her head to one side. She had close-cropped white hair, a high contrast to her warm skin, and crinkled eyes that were grey in the artificial light.

"Yeah, I know it sounds daft, but I kept seeing the same colours of carpets, and there's no floor numbers on the doors, so I can't tell where I am. I should have been down at reception by now but I'm...wherever I am."

"Oh, you must have ended up on the staff stairs." Her eyebrows popped up. "Easy done. You want to go for the steps at that end, they're the public ones." She pointed down the longer corridor that joined with the one Stephanie had entered, to a heavy wooden door.

"I didn't realise there were two sets of steps," Stephanie said.

11

"Guests aren't meant to be on the staff ones. If you take that door and go down one flight you'll be in a wide hall, you want to take the double doors opposite you on the right-hand side."

"Great, thank you." Stephanie nodded to the throng of women as she passed them and walked to the dark door. The architecture in this place made no sense. How had she missed there were two sets of stairs? Another one of those older things, wanting to keep the quirky bits of the building. It was giving her a headache.

She pushed through the door and was met by a cool rush of air, these stairs broader than before. The same red carpet as the corridor ran down them, tramped down by many feet before hers, and the chatter of voices drifted up. This was a bit more like it.

She started down them, following the stairs through a dogleg corner and into the broad, square hall promised. It was a shock to the senses: the floor was white tile with black inlay to create an intricate, circled symbol, the centre a mass of triangular patterns that left the impression of a constellation. The walls were a cool blue, not too different to the level her room had been on, with bright lights to make up for the lack of windows. Corridors ran off each corner, the one dead ahead leading to another set of stairs and the one to her right a third set. She went towards the one diagonally opposite her, the double doors tall and thinner than the others.

A lift exit was in the centre of the opposite wall too, an ornately carved guard screen covering the access. It was the same brass as the button panels in the main hotel, shiny at contact points like the handle. She paused in front of it, examining the metalwork. Some bars had vine and flower designs, the buds just opening or in full bloom and ready to spill down. It was obvious why they'd keep that piece; the artistry was clear, even to her hungover mind. She fingered over one of the opening blossoms, the metal warming under her touch, even as a sharp edge pricked her skin. Shaking herself off she stepped back, going for the doors.

They shared the same brass as the lift, the opaque glass a surprise for safety doors. All corridors had safety doors now. You could have seen someone moving through them, just not who it was. They'd probably adapted it.

She pushed one open to meet a wide corridor, curving round at the end. The floor here was tile too, bright white with black borders, and her footsteps bounced back at her.

It was the first time she'd seen art on the walls in the hotel—crowding the space. There was a mishmash of paintings and smaller sculptures sat on display tables, like an untended gallery. Made sense they'd be in the public areas, rather than people's rooms where they might get damaged. Or stolen.

She rounded the corner into a vast room. It would have been a suite in somewhere fancier than here, with open brick walls and a lot of dark wood accents. A long fireplace dominated the far wall, with a burning stack ready to be lit, and a large bed sat against the nearest wall, made up to be used. A short bar occupied the corner diagonally opposite to where she stood, inviting exploration. A further door seemed to lead into what looked like a bathroom tucked into a stumpy corridor.

The real oddity was the place itself: all the bits she could see were on one level but the more she got to the centre of the room the floor stratified, sinking down in two broad, square stone layers that almost created a seating area. They led to a large, square hole in the centre. It was about as wide as a door, maybe a little more, the edges reinforced with a carved border, and it looked deep. She peered at it a little, stepping up to the edge of the sandstone. There weren't any visible internal edges, no way to get an idea of how far down it went unless she got down another level. Which she absolutely was not doing.

Turning on her heel she went back down the corridor, her case's wheels a loud accompaniment as she marched towards the doors, thoroughly ruffled. She didn't know what this was, but she knew a bad idea when she saw one.

CHAPTER 3

- -

S he hurried through the doors, jumping to see the hall filled with people, a mass of bodies milling around with carts and buckets, arms full of sheets. Stephanie faltered, uncertain where they'd come from in the minutes it had taken her to walk into that room and back again.

The walls were coated in rippling, milk white scum and streaks of green rot, the floor stained with rusted brown lines over the tiles. No one looked at her, all eyes down to focus on the ground, and there was a dull roaring like a train coming along the tracks.

"What the fuck?" Her shoulders came up around her ears as the sound got louder. She spotted the older woman from earlier, who had pointed her down the corridor, and darted forward to grab her arm. "What's going on?" The space had started to shake, like an earthquake was going to happen. They were in *Scotland*, for goodness' sake.

"We're ghosts."

Stephanie blinked, sweat prickling along the nape of her neck. She took her hand back, fist clenching around her bag strap. "That's not what I asked."

"It's what you should have, though," the woman said with a kind smile, patting Stephanie's arm. "The hotel likes you. He'll be here soon to let you know what's happening."

"Why does it look like this?" She pointed to the creeping rot, the discoloured floor.

"That's because you're outside of the suite," called a male voice. Stephanie jumped back, closer to the doors. Thomas, the chipper concierge, was standing in the middle of the ornate patterns on the floor. His tan was gone, skin now wax white, and his shirt streaked with a dark stain that bloomed from the centre of his chest. The swarm of figures parted so there was a clear line between him and Stephanie, like fish parting before a shark.

"Suite?"

"As Martha was saying, thank you, Martha." He glared at the older woman and she hurried off, giving Stephanie another small smile. "The hotel likes you. The Basker has a wide and proud history, and occasionally it selects souls for service. You have the honour of being one of those chosen."

A crack like thunder punctuated his words, and Stephanie flinched. "What the fuck does that mean? Why does it sound like it's falling down?"

"Your living presence on this side of the veil is difficult to maintain. The hotel is doing its best to accommodate you, but the suite is the safest place for you to stay. If you remain in this area, the facade will crumble, and you'll be lost to the void."

"The void as in that hole in there?" She pointed at the doors, yanking on her bag strap like it was a life ring.

"No, that's the heart of the hotel. The void is that." He swung his right arm, pointing to the stairs directly across from her. The hotel was flaking, the slime and mould buckling to fade into blackness. It lurched forward, swallowing the steps up to the edge of the tiled floor with a screeching crunch.

"And if that gets me?"

"You'll simply cease to be. No afterlife, no moving on, or whatever your religion of choice may prescribe. Simply nothing."

"What the fuck?"

"When you choose to join the hotel, you'll be part of something much larger than yourself. A purpose. More than most get in their lifetime, never mind after death."

"It's a hotel. How much of a cause can there be in being bricks?"

"Ah, the Basker is much more than that. You'll see once you join. The best way of doing that is giving yourself over to the heart of the hotel. You can lower yourself in, though I recommend jumping. Fingernails aren't meant to support bodyweight and instinct is a powerful thing." He held his left hand up, the middle three fingers missing their nails: the stumps were bloody, dark purple with bruising.

She shook her head. "You went into the pit."

"Eventually. I tried to kill myself first." He touched the hand to his chest, the fingertips coming away scarlet. "The void was unappealing."

"Let me go."

"It's quite beyond my choice to do anything like that," he said with a bright smile, only slightly flinching when another burst of sound ripped through the hall. A large crack appeared across the floor, the tiles tumbling down into dust.

"This is insane."

"I suggest you go back inside and think about what you want to do. You can join with the hotel, or kill yourself. Or join the void. The hotel is patient, it'll give you time. You can use the suite programme to make your stay as comfortable as possible meantime."

"What happens if you kill yourself?"

"I didn't wait to find out. Practically, we use the bodies for meat unless there's something that spoils them."

"Glad I went for the vegetarian breakfast this week," Stephanie said.

"It pleased me you followed my recommendations. I'd love to have you as an understudy."

"Fuck off."

"You should go back inside the suite. You're putting quite a strain on the hotel."

The back wall buckled, folding in on itself with an inhuman groan. Stephanie grabbed her case and went back through the doors, slamming them closed. The thundering sounds stopped and she let herself slide down, ass bumping into the cool tile as her legs splayed out.

This was insane. Maybe this was a hallucination, a terrible reaction to something in the drink last night. Or she was locked in a nightmare, one of those episodes you got when your sleep went fucked up. People joked about sleep paralysis demons; she'd found sleep paralysis hell.

She took her phone out and found it was still on, but no signal or internet. Great. She let herself dip forward, head onto her knees. Swallowing against the urge to cry, she breathed through her nose, trying to get as much oxygen to her brain as possible. There had to be a logical way to deal with this.

Standing up, she looked around her, spotting a set of buttons on her left—just like the lift panel—a coiling work of metal with shiny, creamy buttons beside a list of words. They were stacked up on top of each other like a menu: *bath, fire, library, loveseat, art, windows, bar, music.* The options for fire, windows and bar were depressed already.

Hesitantly she put her finger to *music*, pushing it in. It clicked into place with the sound of rolling dice, and she heard music start up in the room at the end of the hall, something classical on a piano. She pushed it again and it popped out, the music stopping.

Taking her case she went back down the corridor, lingering at the threshold. The floor was treated wood at this part, she'd missed that earlier, and the descending levels were a tan sandstone. It was a bit of a clash, but the colours worked. Somehow.

The bed was still there, king sized with black sheets. She could go and lie down on it, stare at the too-white ceiling and see if she woke up from this. She could run back through the doors at the other end of the corridor, see how far she could get. Vanishing staircases and screaming metal made her rethink that, stepping into the room instead.

Tugging her case up onto the bed, she sat down beside it. She didn't know what to do. She always unpacked if she was staying more than one day. Slowly, she started to cry.

Chapter 4

- -

Stephanie stood beside the suite doors, looking over the list. She pushed the button for *bath* and heard same the rattling drop followed by loud swoop, like the curtains closing in a theatre. The light from the end of the corridor dimmed, then rallied.

She walked back to the room, peering round the corner to check what had happened. A huge, claw-footed bath sat where the bar had been, shiny gold taps hooked over one long side. The fire had also started up, a healthy glow painting the white tub with a creamy sheen. Sticking as close to the wall as she could, glaring at the pit when she passed, she went to inspect it.

It was already full, and loaded with bubbles, steam skimming up. The smell of jasmine and frangipani rose with the curling wisps, and her heart lurched at the scent of home. Those were her bath oils, the expensive ones people got you as gifts because you didn't spend that much on yourself. Exactly what she'd want after travelling all day. Trailing her fingers through the bubbles, she savoured the heat, just too hot, the sort that made your muscles unknot and your mind quieten.

She missed the bar.

Abandoning the bath, she went back to the corridor, checking over her other options. She hit *bar* again, ignoring the swishing noise, then pressed *loveseat*. There was a solid thump, like something heavy being dropped. Coming back into the room, she met a low two-seater sofa, decked out in red velvet and contrasting gold cushions, sat with its back to the windows. And the bar was back.

She went to that first, checking the options. Two stools stood behind the bar, looking out over the room, spaced a bit too close to be practical. There was a silent fridge with a solid door, well stocked when she opened it, and a selection of spirits in a small optic set above that. She had the run of wines and fizz, a few types of juices, and a small bowl of red fruits nestled in the front. Plucking a bottle of Moscato out of the back, she popped the cork and poured a glass, taking both with her as she crossed before the fire—still burning—to the loveseat. There was no table, just a view across the room to the bar and bathroom. And the pit.

Swigging the sparkling wine back, she winced at the sweetness but kept going, emptying the glass in three deep swallows. She poured another and sat heavily on the seat, looking over the dark brick walls. They weren't dramatic enough to be called red as blood; theirs was a more earthy tone, almost like the old sandstone you saw in some cathedrals. Standing, she ran a finger over the nearest wall, the gritty residue confirming her suspicions.

The city had used a lot of sandstone in the industrial revolution. This must be in one of the old parts of the hotel. Or wherever this was.

Thomas had called it the veil. Or something, she should have paid more attention. She drank more wine to drown her panic. Would she have an eternal hangover? The last one had drained away with her tears, leaving her flat and listless. At least the sugar should perk her up.

The windows caught her eye, the space behind them white as cigarette smoke. She'd thought they were the same as the doors, frosted glass, but it wasn't that. Wandering closer as she drank, she saw fog outside of them, twirling and spreading like waves. The sashes were like the windows in her hotel room, the same little metal hoops on the lower framing. She set the glass and bottle down, then pulled the window up as far as she could.

The air that spilled in was cooler, just enough to give the dampness of the mist. She stuck her head out, leaning her hands on the stone sill, loose grit biting into her skin as she let her weight shift. Closing her eyes, she strained to hear any noises below her, or above. Anything.

Her face grew damp with droplets of vapor, but nothing else came: no sounds of the street, no traffic, not even the fucking pigeons roosting.

Ducking back inside, she sucked her lower lip, the hot itch of panic creeping up her skin. There couldn't just be *nothing*. She grabbed the bottle and leant out again, holding it as far from the building as she could before letting go. It vanished into the fog below, and she watched the white swirl like milk poured into tea. Holding her breath, she strained to listen, waiting for the crash of that jewel green glass hitting pavement. She had to breathe again when her lungs were burning and her eyes watered, letting her head drop low.

Sniffing, she went back inside, closing the window with a dull thud. The glass was just as cool as the air outside when she rested her forehead against it, breath fogging. This didn't make sense. This was some H. H. Holmes *bullshit*.

Turning from the window she flopped onto the loveseat, shoving the cushions aside. One tipped over, bouncing back into her lap, and she seized it, squeezing until her nails hurt. The pain was good, solid, a focus against the screaming in her brain.

She hiccupped around a sob, throwing the cushion away from her. It bounced off one of the seating levels, tumbling from the upper edge into the lower and skidding end over end into the pit. No noise from that either.

Morbid curiosity made her rise from the seat, stretching her neck to see if anything changed. There'd been no sound, but maybe dust motes? She stood on the upper layer of the room, almost on tiptoes, to check. She still remembered how to sweep for activity; that shit never went far below the surface.

She stepped down onto the first set of tan stone, waiting there for a beat lest it triggered anything. Satisfied nothing was about to drop from under her, she sat down, crossed legged, at the edge.

Nothing except cool air came up to meet her, the darkness swamping everything below the stone. She let her legs unfold and kicked her heels against the block, chewing the inside of her mouth. She wished she'd kept the bottle now, for courage as much as experiment.

The pit didn't seem to have walls, just a sheer chasm of blackness, which didn't make her confident about standing on the bottom layer. She did though, keeping the back of her legs tight against the stone so she could stand and lean over, stretching to see as far into the gap as she could.

The sandstone scratched her calves through the leggings as she inched around the perimeter. Aside from the designs around the edges there was nothing to give her an idea of craft or carving, no overhanging rocks or visible slope leading away. She knelt, tucked into one corner with her ribs pressed to the upper layer. Tense as a rabbit and ready to bolt, she held her hand out over the hole.

Nothing. The chill continued to slip through her fingers like the absence of a lover, but nothing surged to grab her. She pulled her arm back, curling the hand close to her chest. There was no noise in the room except her breathing. Not even the fire seemed to make a sound.

She tucked her knees underneath herself and leaned forward a little, testing how far down she could see. It just kept going, like staring down into the ocean at night, the layers of light vanishing into inky mystery. She sniffed, edging closer in increments in case she could catch anything from the little breeze. It smelled like stale air, the way you got in houses that had been left uninhabited too long. Emptiness.

Shaking herself, she stood up, dusting off the granules across her leggings. Everything she touched seemed to come off around her, little dustings of the hotel clinging to her skin and clothes. She had no intention of letting it creep up on her like that, though. Turning to step out of the seating area she froze, eyes on the loveseat.

Two cushions sat side by side on the low piece, gold thread shiny and bright. Identical to when it came into the room. She swallowed, working her tongue against the top of her mouth as she glanced back between the cushions and the pit. There hadn't been the sound of dice, or the heavy thump she'd heard before. Nothing other than her heavy heartbeat.

She scrambled away from both seat and pit, making for the bar.

CHAPTER 5

Stephanie didn't have the patience for real cocktails, so she made mimosas with the Moscato and orange juice, knocking them back quicker than a boozy brunch.

It was easy to drink, and she worked through a bottle, resisting the urge to throw that in the pit and see what reappeared. She started on clear spirits next.

Gin went with most fruit, so she mixed it with cranberry juice and a dash of orange, and shots from the cap when the presence of the pit loomed too bright in her mind. Perched on the bar stool she watched it, hands shaking as she tipped the alcohol past her lips.

It dimly occurred to her that she should eat something, lest she end up throwing up all her efforts. There was no food in the room except fruit for the bar, and much as she loved cherries, they would not protect her investment in drunken oblivion.

She leant against the wall as she made her way to the corridor, hesitating at the bed. She'd left her case on it and had a giddy impulse to open it and tip herself inside. Surround herself with her clothes and the feel of home, to tug the lid over her head and hide from the insanity.

Her head swam a little as she sat down on the bed like a sack, lolling back to look at the ceiling. There was no button to change that. No beams to hang yourself from, either. She should have left the music on, something to distract from the painful silence. Her thoughts drifted to the pit, drawing everything down to it.

Yanking one of her travel jumpers out of the case, she tugged it over her head, curling in on herself as she twisted it on. It smelled like the cats. Her throat clenched at the thought of them and the anger that spilled out with her tears got her up again, off the bed and stumbling along the corridor. She paused at the door, slapping her cheeks to sober up a bit.

Cracking the door open, she saw the milling scrum of ghosts, the afterimage equal parts fear and alcohol. Spirits and spirits. Thomas was standing in the middle like a conductor, watching her.

"Have you decided already?" he asked.

"Do you just hang out here?"

"I'm able to be present in multiple situations at once. A gift given by the hotel." He nodded to the tiled floor.

"Neat trick," she said, stepping out and leaning against the door. "There's no button for food, or a kitchen. Do I ask you for that?"

"You don't need to eat."

"It's rude to call a woman fat." A choked laugh escaped her.

"You misunderstand me. There's no need for food here. The alcohol, while enjoyable, is not necessary either. I found it helped."

"How long were you in there?" She folded her arms, stealing glances around. The rot had curled over the place as they spoke, lurid streaks of green and scummy orange rippling over the walls like sunflowers chasing noon. A low rumble rattled along the floor.

"Time has no real meaning in there. You entered it hours ago, but a different time has passed over with the living."

Stephanie blinked, the idea settling over her like spiderwebs. "That's not an answer."

"Days bleed together. I read all the books in the library more times that I could remember. There's some wonderful works."

"Then you went into the pit?"

"I stabbed myself with the ice pick first. But yes." He spread his nail-less fingers apart and sank them into holes at his chest, two knuckles deep. Stephanie retched, gripping her throat as she pushed herself back against the door.

"That's not how you tend a wound."

Thomas shrugged, letting his hand drop. The fingers were slick with dark blood, brown as coffee. "I don't have to worry about that. The Basker makes such things unnecessary."

"Right."

A loud crunch rippled between them, the stairs across from Stephanie cracking into two. The half closest to the wall fizzed into nothing, swallowed into darkness.

Thomas sighed. "Go back inside. The void hasn't settled since your last excursion; it's slow abate."

"Why's it even there?"

"Why is chaos anywhere?" Thomas glanced over at the advancing decay. The hall shook, spores of the rot sprinkling from the ceiling. "I could explain parts of it to you, but you'll know once you join us."

"Not happening." She groped around behind her for the handle, palms slick with cold sweat. Once found, she toppled back inside as the ground began to crack, landing on her ass in the hallway. The door swung shut, removing Thomas from view.

She drooped back onto the floor; head spinning and stomach tight. Rolling onto her side lest the inevitable occur, she wondered idly if choking on her vomit counted as killing herself.

Sitting up, she rocked onto her knees, tugging herself to standing with the help of the door. Her vision swam a little as she looked at the buttons, jabbing the one for *music* and eyeing the others. Nothing called to her, so she turned and went back into the suite, wandering over to the bar as the piano songs started.

She stared into the fridge, barely surprised to see the fresh Moscato bottles. Her hand froze as she reached for one, an alternative idea springing up. Closing the door, she went towards the bathroom, nudging the door open with her foot and clipping the light switch.

It had a long, trim window that reminded her of castle ramparts, no hoop to open it, and a huge glass shower with a square water panel at the top. The light was diffused, the luxurious warm glow of suites and spas, and a stack of towels sat in a neat pile beside a broad basin that looked deep enough to drown someone. An enormous mirror was above it, ringed with bulbs and broad enough to take up most of the cream wall. It was the first mirror she'd seen in the suite, none lurking with the art in the corridor, and her reflection was a pale, sweaty mess.

She loitered at the door, etching the layout into her mind. The lack of toilet lingered like a presence, the space where it should be taken up by a tall cabinet made of ash-washed wood. It really brought the room together.

A shower would be good. She'd skipped hers this morning because of the hangover. It would be normal, washing and drying off away from the pit.

She stepped back and grabbed her toiletries from her case, then slipped in, leaving the door open lest the entire suite change while she washed her hair. There were toiletries there for her, ornate containers of mysterious liquid that shone like pearls when she cracked the lid open. She sniffed, a shudder running through her—ginger and black pepper, like she had at home. The cats stayed away when she first used it, too potent for them.

The thought of the cats made her face spasm, a grimace of pain reflected in the glowing mirror. She screwed her eyes shut, pounding a fist into her hipbone to distract herself from the twist in her chest. It was a bad coping mechanism, one she'd tried to leave behind on tour, but the pain radiated out from her hits and grounded her *there*, mind narrowed to the throbbing ache in the bone and muscle. Would she bruise? If you could kill yourself, then a bruise was likely. Should check in the morning.

She stripped quickly, tossing her clothes into the ridiculous basin. The piano music drifted in like an afterthought, curling through the room. The song might have been different; she wasn't sure. She turned the water on. It came down in a cloudburst, steam tumbling over itself like the fog outside. It occurred to her briefly that she could bring a bottle in there with her, but that was straying into alcoholism by default. Instead, she grabbed her toiletries and got into the wide glass box, turning up the water until it nearly burned.

Her mind drifted back to the bath, the delicious scent of the steam and bubbles. Soaking in front of the pit seemed ridiculous. Especially at the cost of the bar. Thomas had mentioned an ice pick; she didn't have that in her fridge. She'd not even looked for ice. The fruit was pre-sliced, so no knife there either.

After scrubbing herself raw, she traced a finger from shoulder to elbow, feeling the muscle of her bicep dip and shift under the pressure. She felt real. The raw sensitivity left by hot water and vicious cleaning was there, exacerbated by the steam. She washed her hair out of habit rather than desire, turning the shower off once the suds were gone.

Stepping out of the glass, she grabbed two towels and tipped forward, briefly squeezing the water out of her hair. Twisting it round itself to keep it in place, she came back up, flipping the towel over so it ran down her back. Grabbing the larger bath sheet, she wrapped it around herself, turning to the fogged mirror and jumping like someone had doused her with ice. Her legs went out from under her, and she landed on the slick floor with a thump, the air going out of her.

It's too late once you're here. Find your own way out or join it. I'm sorry.

It was written repeatedly, filling the glass in precise, fingertip script. Stephanie lost count of how many lines there were, vision blurring as tears slipped down her face. She scrabbled back from the mirror until she met a wall. Glancing around, she had a brief impression of a shape in the shower: a shock of blond hair, a slumped body, legs sticking out of the door, a flood of red coating the fuzzed chest and pooling in the bottom tray, the glint of a shaving razor shining out of the crimson. It vanished as she wiped her face; the liquid on her hands coming away mercifully clear.

She shoved against the door, flipping onto her knees to crawl out of the room and retreat to the bed. Her throat was tight, the burn of tears and more screams tangled in her chest. Climbing onto the covers, she got herself to the centre, tugging her knees up against her chest as she watched the door. Nothing came but wisps of steam, curling and rising like birds in mist. She'd seen that before: flitting shapes billowing and swooping in breaking dawns. Check-ins and radio crackle.

Her stomach twisted at the vestige of the body in there, whoever the man had been. Neat handwriting. A straight razor.

It had gone dark by the time she unfolded from the bed in slight movements, towels cold on her skin and the wall lights flickering into life. No monster grabbed for her ankles when she stood. The bathroom door was still open, and she hovered just before it, scanning the room. Any steam had long since cleared out and the narrow window was as dim. The shower was clean.

Stepping in, she dashed to her clothes, scooping them to her chest and hugging them close. The writing on the mirror was gone, and she leaned in, looking for smears. The glass was clean, plain; no sign of the previous message.

She pulled back but paused at the legs still showing in the bottom corner of the mirror. Her heart thumped against her ribs once, heavy as a horse kick, and she broke out in a cold sweat that soaked into her towel. Keeping her eyes fixed on the corner, she turned her head just a little, enough that she could look to the shower.

Nothing.

Looking back to the mirror she could clearly see them: the blond down of hair catching the light, knees scuffed. Going up onto tiptoes, the shower tray came into view, full of coagulated blood. She retched, turning away from the mirror to strip and redress. She didn't bother brushing her hair, instead grabbing the toiletries, and leaving the room.

She dumped the shower cap on the bed and went back to the bar, mixing a shot of each clear spirit together then topping up orange juice, and plucking a bottle of rosé out of the fridge. She tossed the pink bottle onto the covers as she went past, sipping the too-potent cocktail and shuddering along the corridor.

Off went the music with a vicious jab as she looked at her other options. She pressed the button for *library* and saw the lights in the room dim, a grinding noise like heavy rocks moving together rippling out.

The lights came back as she walked to the suite, her suspicions confirmed—a set of four bookcases replaced the bar, stood two abreast and tucked into the corner. They were taller than her, a little set of wooden stairs nestled into the crook of them for reaching the top shelves, and they were crammed *full*.

There wasn't an inch of free space, the gaps between the shelf and the top of books stuffed with smaller volumes, some turned onto their sides and stacked like receipts when they were too tall to fit otherwise. They were all black, in contrast to the rich, dark wood of the cases, all the spines adorned with golden writing in differing sizes and length.

They drew her over, the familiarity—normality—of the books reaching out to her. Pausing beside the bed, she knocked the rest of her too-many-mixed drink back, shaking her head against the kick and tossing the glass into the pit.

She snatched the wine bottle and continued, winding slightly as she kept one hand on the wall to balance against the onslaught of spirits.

Impulsive move: she'd had too much. She knew how to do damage control drinking and this was not that.

"I should have a straw for this, one of those stupid metal ones," she said, leaning against the wall as she fiddled with the bottle screwcap. Closing one eye to help her focus, she undid the foil wrapping and dropped it beside the bed, twisting the top loose and taking a quick gulp. It was a summery drink, cherry and strawberry sweet on her tongue.

Her mouth felt thick with the sugar and she stayed on the wall for a beat, letting her worldview catch up with her movements. The bookcases were only at the other side of the room. It would take a handful of paces to get there. She slid down the wall instead, feet unsteady as she gripped the bottle with white knuckles. Leaning against the bed once she reached the floor, her gaze settled on the pit, just the lip of it visible from where she sat.

It was darker than the windows outside, heavy and yearning. Demanding. Thomas's fingers were still bloody from holding onto the edge. He said she should just jump rather than lower in. Humans clawed for any way to survive.

Bringing the bottle to her lips, she took two long drags, knocking her head against the wall as she leant back too quickly. It was a distant sort of impact, more an awareness than any genuine pain. She fixed her eyes on the pit again, and waited.

CHAPTER 6

Someone was whispering. She'd fallen asleep, having crawled under the duvet after the wine was finished. Now she could hear a voice.

Blinking sleep out of her eyes, she sat up in the covers. The room was dark, just the soft glow of the dying fire to see by; there were lamps close by, but she didn't want to tip off whoever was there. Her head still swam with her drinking and light would probably be unhelpful there too. Instead, she crept forward, hands and knees on the bed so she didn't make a noise.

Her eyes adjusted to the dark as she lurked there, low against the covers like her body still knew how to do, until she could trace the shapes of the room—the bathroom door, the library corner, the tall windows. The descending stones. The corridor was dark, and the whispering was coming from inside the room, soft as a babbling stream. The fire still gave just enough light to cast shadows, and she couldn't see anyone, but that meant nothing here.

Slipping off the bed in cautious, padding steps, she inched around the side nearest the door, slipping in front of the loveseat to get towards the fire. It had a poker beside it. Her heart was thudding, bound to be give her away, and she held her breath as she passed the pit.

Her mental location was off, and she put one foot too far wide—plummeting forward as her bodyweight tipped and sent her sprawling across the sunken area. She slapped the stone against the pain in her front, breasts squashed and sore from being landed on, breathing open-mouthed to quieten her gasps. It bloody hurt, and the back of her leg was throbbing from being scraped against the stone as she went down, thankfully catching herself before bloodying her face. She pushed herself up and twisted so she could rub the skin, checking for scratches.

The sound was louder now—hissing words picking up an insistence that had been lacking. Stephanie swallowed, deafening in her ears, and strained to listen.

It was the pit. Dark whispers were drifting up, curling and twisting like wind in the autumn. She could feel it creeping over her hand as she gingerly held it out, palm licked with a dampness separate from the cool, flowing air. She leaned forward just an inch, back coming away from the stone, tilting her head to one side to see if she could hear it properly.

They were indistinct words, tripping over each other like there were multiple voices. It was layered, repetitive, a husky scratch against her ear. If she could just get closer, it would be clear, surely. If she could lean nearer.

She curled into herself, lowering down onto the second layer and sitting on her ankles, folding down so her sore chest was against her thighs. This close the air stirred her hair, still damp from all day in the towel. The words poured, flowing like water as she gradually shifted her weight forward, palms flat against the stone to aid retreat.

Her head was almost over the pit now. The carved edges itched under her fingertips—the worked grooves and loose grains coarse as sandpaper. It would hurt if she tried to claw them. Her hands shifted forward a touch, her first knuckles slithering over the edge, so she could really hold on.

It was thicker than she thought; the stone continuing down for half a hand-span. She splayed her fingers to give the best grip, most control, thumbs almost touching as she lowered further. The lip of the pit beckoned: a contrast in shades of darkness between the shadowed room and the breathing absence. The dying embers made it more obvious, the quick, fluid light of the low fire giving a wavering pulse to the black. Closing her eyes, she went just a little further, slipping her face close to the coolness and holding her breath.

Her hair slid free from her ear and dangled into the space, swaying in the stream of words. The tone had changed again, the raspy burble slower now, coaxing her to sink lower. A breath of cold air brushed against her cheek and her eyes opened, turning on impulse to see what caused the new draft.

A pair of wide, golden eyes met her gaze, and fingers slid up from the edge of the pit to join with hers, snaking between her rigid grip to give a small squeeze. They were cold and damp, like leather after rain. Something sharp pressed at the webs of her skin—enough pressure to show they could pierce through but didn't.

Those eyes were so gold: the whole oval flooded like a pair of amulets settled in black velvet. Slowly, what could have been lips—or could have been yellowed, folded leaves caught on the breeze, or could have been streams of molten metal burning up in the chill dark—drifted up to join the eyes, the soft impression of a face pushing into form.

It was barely even there except it *was*, ebbing and flowing as if on waves, only those eyes holding her. The lips were chanting, syncing up with the noise that crashed over her like she was a pebble on the shore. Stephanie spoke with it, mouthing along, in a pathetic echo.

"I'm sorry. Join me. I'm sorry. Join me." She choked around the words, the floating imitation face nodding, surging forward as they spoke together. They could kiss, they were so close, the soft promise of those burning lips only a breath away.

Shaking her head, a sob rippling through her like the thrum of electricity, she pulled back, tugging her fingers free. The face rose after her and she scrabbled up the stone levels, towards the fire.

Leaning against the fireplace, she found the poker. The metal worked in twisting lines like a barber's pole, the handle a thicker, textured segment that would sit in her palm. It would be easy to drive it through whatever that was, in there, to pluck the poker from the hanger and beat it over and over until the gold was dented and broken.

She buckled down onto her knees, catching herself on her hands before her face landed in the embers. Gagging, she vomited, the bitter tang of old alcohol mixing with acrid smoke. She threw up until there was no more to come, until she was spitting foam and bile.

Her throat was raw, throbbing, the sharp taste of blood clear. She wiped her face with the back of her hand, tipping to lean against the stone fireplace. Her head rocked back, face to the ceiling. The whispering had calmed down again—the indistinct murmur of a stream rather than roaring waves.

The bed was against the opposite wall, the pit between her and unconsciousness. Sleeping in front of the fire seemed perversely open. No cover. You always needed cover.

She opened her eyes and leant over, knocking the poker down, dragging it closer one handed. The weight was good in her hand. Steady.

Getting up with shaking legs, she breathed deep, hugging the metal pole to her chest. It was warm along one side, a line of heat glowing along her sternum and stomach.

The loveseat route was too treacherous, so she turned to go towards the library corner instead, glancing to the pit. A sliver of the face was peering at her, those eyes just above the ledge. It couldn't have seen her when she was kneeling before the fire. The stone would have been in the way.

She stepped closer to the bookcases and the gaze followed her, the small shift of the eyes matching her pace. The poker was heavy against her sore chest, and she shifted it, tucking it close to her left, against her ribs. She rolled her shoulders and moved across the space in quick steps, watching out of the edge of her sight as the face tracked her. Nothing but the tip of the head and the eyes were out, bobbing as if on water. Letting out a burning breath as she reached the bed she stopped, turning to look at the pit: the eyes were there, unblinking.

She scrabbled under the covers, tugging the metal rod with her as she yanked the pillows down too. The duvet settled, heavy as the rain that had haunted her trip, and the whispers still burbled on.

Settling halfway down the mattress, she tugged the other pillow closer, boxing herself in so the poker could lie beside her like a knight's sword. She curled up, folding her arms under her head for support and letting one hand slip onto the metal handle.

It was dark enough that she didn't need to close her eyes—could tell herself if they closed it would make no difference. It was hot enough with the heat of her breath and the low, radiating promise of the poker, that it didn't matter if those cold, gold eyes came after her.

Her tears were hotter than the metal when they started.

CHAPTER 7

There was a stack of books waiting for her the next morning, set on the top of the ladder. She walked past them, brushing her teeth on her knees.

When she finished, she slunk back towards the door on her knees, avoiding the mirror. She was no company for dead men. Two steps into the suite she found it was back in order; the bed made, the poker hanging beside the prepared fireplace, her case stood beside her pillows, closed.

Blinking away the shock, she shook with a fine tremble of cold, wrapping her arms around her torso as she took in the rest of the room. The loveseat was still there, cushions neat as sentries, and the gaps on the bookshelf shouted like missing piano teeth. The pit still waited for her in its sunken centre, though no eyes sought her out.

Going to the bed, she crawled over it to get her case, flipping it open to change her clothes. She should unpack. No point taking the electronics out—her phone was still on, but no use, no connections. The background of her and Jenny was a bittersweet comfort, and she shoved it back into the compartment with her work clothes.

Tucking the case under the bed, she went back to the books, squatting down to look at the titles. A mix of plays, poetry, and prayers awaited her, stacked up like stones on a beach. The urge to knock them over like her cats would surged, but she grabbed the bottom of the pile and lifted the lot to her chest, standing with the movement. She was still bruised from last night, but nothing more than a dull ache.

Walking over to the bed, she dumped the books onto the duvet, then went down the corridor and hit the buttons for *music* and *bar*, listening for a beat to see if the accompaniment would drown out the swooping. It didn't; the heavy sound came first.

Her finger lingered over the *windows* option for a moment, but she pulled back, unsure she could tolerate whatever replaced the false light. She had no way to mark time other than that, her wristwatch with her phone in the pocket of shame. Being totally without reference was unconscionable.

The music was almost jazz, something a little more dirge like than she would usually pick. She hovered beside the door, looking at the thin strips of glass for a long breath. Her hand drifted up to trace the metal lines on the opposite side, fingers snaking along the shadows. No. She'd already decided she was no company for dead men, stationary or taunting.

Instead, she went back down the corridor. The art had changed: the paintings larger, taking up more space with smaller gaps. The scenes were water based—boats tossed on the storm, Poseidon rising out of the surf with wrathful eyes. She felt them on her like a brand.

Coming back into the room, she went directly to the bar and opened the fridge. Once again a series of dark-green bottles were lined up, flanked by pink, then the vibrant juices. The fruit sat at the front, ready sliced. A row of metal straws lay before the fruit container like bodies at a vigil. She picked a bottle of Moscato and a glass, taking them back to bed with her.

Hair of the dog and poetry seemed like a delightful combination, so she sifted through the books, picking out a volume of Neruda—*Twenty Love Poems; And a Song of Despair*. She poured a glass of sparkling wine, taking the bottle with her as she settled on the loveseat, tucking one leg under herself to nestle into the corner.

Wine for breakfast was messy, and this fizzy, sweet stuff tickled her nose as she took a sip. Then another. A glass or three should be enough to keep the headache at bay, and she could try to tackle a plan for what to do once she was a bit calmer.

She opened the book and found "A Song of Despair" was the first poem in the volume. She sighed, closing the book and laying in on her lap. This was not how the book went. She knew Neruda, had been reading him since she was a closeted teenager *yearning* in her bedroom.

Swirling the glass, she took an overeager gulp, poured herself more wine, set it down beside the loveseat. Settling her hands over the book, she closed her eyes for a beat, muttering a prayer to the universe that she was wrong.

Taking the book up again, she opened it in the middle, eyeing the bar before she looked down. "A Song of Despair" was on both pages. She dropped it and screamed, her head knocking into the back of the sofa, before she grabbed the glass, knocking it back in two deep swallows.

Flipping the book closed, she stared at the ceiling as she played with the now empty glass, rolling the stem between her fingertips. Having another would be beyond medicinal and onto a buzz, pushing herself into the haze and confidence of intoxication. She put the glass down and picked up the bottle instead, pushing off the seat.

She tossed the poetry into the pit as she went back to the bed, sitting heavily on it as she picked up the collection of plays—Shakespeare. It was a hefty book, the spine as broad as four fingers. She set it in the crook of her knee and pursed her lips, gripping the bottleneck tightly.

Opening the cover, she saw the full list of plays, chronically ordered in neat, square type. She ran her finger along the dotted line between the names and the page number for *A Midsummer Night's Dream*, a play she had done to death in secondary school. She could still quote lines.

Cracking the book open at what should have been the start of the play, she was instead halfway through *Titus Andronicus*, too late in the collection. She flipped through the pages, chasing where the play should be. They slid straight into *Julius Caesar*, then into *Hamlet*. She closed it.

The prayer book was next, and she drank straight from the bottle before she dared turn to that. The cover did not indicate the denomination, just a gold cross embossed into the front, so it could have a variety of things waiting for her.

The funeral rites should have been what she expected, but some perverse part of her was hoping things might have been different for a holy book. Not that she was religious. It only took a handful of sermons about how wrong she was before she'd decided the priest didn't know shit about God, and she wasn't going to sit listening to hellfire in a church cold enough to make her breath show.

She pushed it away, flopping backwards onto the covers. No wonder Thomas had thrown himself into the pit if he was reading these all day. Her head swam with the movement and she gripped the bottle, still clenched in her hand.

"Fuck you, by the way," she said to the empty room, a curl of acid creeping up her throat. She swallowed against it, breathing through her nose. "At least give me some of the good misery, like Frankenstein."

The idea of the monstrous story made her giggle, more with her buzz than any actual amusement, and she hiccupped around the creep of vomit and panic. She shook her head and regretted it, the alcoholic fug making the movement double back on itself.

She dragged herself up, away from the reverberation, and folded down on her thighs, covering her face with her hands. This was some bullshit she wasn't ready for. She had abandoned the bottle on the bed but still upright, so she grabbed it and necked the rest, tossing it back onto the covers once empty.

Drinking away the pain was only a temporary option—she knew that—it hadn't worked out in the sandy places, and it didn't work when she came back home, but sometimes temporary measures had a use. It was one she was becoming enamoured with.

She went and propped herself up against the bar, looking over the selection. Her choices were all open: cocktails or straight drink, wine or spirits, garnish or bare.

Going around the counter, she took out the fruit juices and a tall glass, adding two measures of gin before she started mixing. She eyed the vodka for a minute before she settled on a fat cherry instead, skimming it around the lip to leave a sweet, shiny loop.

Hopping up onto the stool she sat and watched the pit, the image of the almost face floating back up behind her eyelids. She dropped a metal straw in the glass and mixed it viciously, taking two deep drinks to ward off the face. The sympathetic, plush mouth.

She worked through two more bottles of wine before she thought she might be sick. The music had turned somewhere between one bottle and the other, back to tinkling piano.

Her brain itched with the thought of the pit. Sat there, vacuous but so demanding, it dominated the room.

Distantly she understood her primal brain recognised it as danger, knew the risk of waiting darkness, but right now she just hated it.

Moving to go to the bathroom, out of habit rather than need, she snagged her foot, landing hard on her knees and she tipped from the stool. Her face was inches from the floor when she blinked realisation into her brain, and her legs throbbed with the impact. The pain reminded her of last night, the injury to her calf. She tugged the legging up to see a bruise, the scrapes red as cat scratches.

That injuries lasted but the room replenished itself kicked around her head like a rat in a cage, something about it pushing against the self-induced haze. She picked herself up using the bar as leverage and stumbled to the bed, grabbing the prayer book.

Her journey along the corridor took longer than it should have, but she did pause halfway along to breathe deep and lean on the wall. Which became sitting against the wall, legs flat on the cool tile as she tried to make some sense of the new art.

It was all stormy seas and angry old gods. A far cry from the detailed, tinkering statues and statement pieces of earlier. There'd been an isolated freedom in those—high contrast and viciously themselves. These were just vicious.

"We can do this, come on." She slapped her palms into her thighs and pushed up, one hand against the wall for reassurance. The door was within reach and she grabbed the handle as if drowning, like it was the only stable thing. Compared to her it was very stable.

Pulling the door open, she peered out, feet planted on the safe side as she gazed around. The hall looked as it should at first, the ornate pattern of black and white beautiful and shiny. No rot or pestilence painted the walls. The only sound was the hum of the lights and her ragged breathing.

The space started to glitch, flickering as she watched: the afterglow of ghosts hovered in and out, switching like a corrupted image. Thomas, standing in the centre of the pattern, was at once there and not, his face curious as she moved her eyes around.

"Can you hear me?" she asked, more experiment than expectation.

No answer came, but the space changed rapidly, alternating between fully decaying and fine, the low rumble of displeasure different to that of the void.

She closed the door, counting to ten before she opened it again. This time she stepped out, one hand firmly on the handle.

The hall was a banquet of wrongness: rot blossoming into spores of white and grey, bright swathes of colour running across the peeling blue paint. The floor was half hidden between the footfall of ghosts and dark stains; the pattern lost except the island of calm surrounding Thomas.

"How does that work, then?" she asked.

His eyes sparkled. "You continue to find new ways to test the veil. Your method is lacking in focus, but effective."

"Good thing I never went into science." The dull grind of the void started up somewhere.

"I'm pleased to see you find the bar adequate."

"Getting drunk seemed a good way to deal with a hangover. Also fuck you for the books." She tossed the prayer book at him, half-hearted anger rising. "No wonder you stabbed yourself."

"I found a lot of comfort in the stories. Maybe your selection was lacking?"

"They were left out for me. I didn't look at them last night."

"Distracted?"

"Drunk. Then distracted when the fucking pit started whispering. Is there a button for that?"

"I can see why Frankie enjoyed your company in the bar. If I didn't have designs on you, I'm sure she'd be delighted to train you." His eyes were still sharp as knives, but there was a new quickness there, like a fox.

"Answer me."

"The pit is the heart of the hotel, it does as it wishes. Your distaste will fade once you join us."

"No chance."

"You might just trip up again." He inspected his dark-stained fingers as if the nails would have grown anew.

"Can you see me in there?"

"No. I'm part of the hotel, so I know."

Stephanie sucked air through her teeth, wrapping her free arm over her abdomen. "There's a lot of company in the room."

"Oh?" Thomas's chest oozed, black blood dripping down his front and onto the tiles below.

"Someone in the shower. And the voice." The void appeared at the top of the stairs in front of her, the consuming darkness peeling the carpet up and splintering the steps.

"The hotel has many ghosts. Some are more active than others. Anything left in the room itself is an indulgence rather than an error." Blood slipped over his teeth now, dribbling past his chin to join that on the tile.

"You didn't mention that."

"I'd hate to spoil the surprise. A concierge must think on her feet."

"Mostly I scream, and drink," Stephanie spat. The heat in her stomach could have been alcohol or anger.

"You'll learn. Most people resist change at first."

Her mind flashed with the glaring faces of the corridor, the resistance to her walking—well, stumbling—along towards the door. "Why is the corridor different?"

"I don't believe it has changed. Are you so deeply indulged you have been seeing things sideways?" His laughter was like battery acid, stinging worse than bile.

"The art, dipshit. The paintings have changed."

"Oh, that." He waved a hand at her, as if wiping her question away. "The hotel has been collecting for hundreds of years. It chooses which items to show as suits its whims."

She opened her mouth to shout at his dismissiveness, but the void leapt forward, surging to the end of the staircase and tearing the wall away behind Thomas. "Fuck."

"You should go back inside."

"What happens if the void reaches you?" Her grip tightened as a sound like shearing ice shook them.

"It won't. It would consume you, though, and I would prefer that doesn't occur. It appears to be a painful death."

"So does stabbing yourself."

CHAPTER 8

The afternoon shifted into evening quickly, the swirling clouds outside losing their pearlescent glow and fading into darkness. Stephanie spent the time drinking and having an argument with herself about a bath.

Being naked in front of the pit seemed obscene. Idiotic.

But she *really* wanted a bath. No way she was getting in that shower again, and the bath smelled like home. It would clear her mind, though, help her shift out of the alcoholic fug that had been enough to blunt the edge of the sharp panic earlier. The room, the hotel, the pit, whatever it was, seemed to like her panicked.

The bath meant going along the corridor again, having all those eyes watch her. Maybe they would approve of her getting closer to water. The hotel might have changed its mind again, changed the pictures, if Thomas was being truthful.

Sighing, she pushed off the seat and stood at the edge of the pit. She toyed with throwing the empty wine bottle down, to see if she heard any smash. It hadn't worked at the window.

Instead, she went over to the bar and pulled out another bottle of fizzy wine. She cradled it in one arm, leaving the empty on the bar, then went to the corridor. Her footsteps were loud as she went, weaving gently to the music.

The art was still glaring at her, but it was easier to go past this time—to shrug off the stares as old, dead rage that lingered.

She got to the buttons, poking the option for *bath* before doubling back. The wine bottle was cool and solid against her side, the weight reassuring—not as good as the poker, but it would do.

Her mental debate on whether or not she would miss the wine if she had to weaponize it lasted until she got into the room and saw the bath stood there, steaming. Her chest ached.

Between her and that absolution, though, sat the pit. Silent throughout the day, its presence remained: a question demanding an answer. Stephanie narrowed her eyes at it, taking a deep breath before she searched for options. The fire was on, had flickered into life at some point she had failed to notice, but there was no fire guard. The room lacked a drying maiden or even a modesty screen.

Opening the wine, she walked around the sunken floor, past the fire, and stood before the bath. She should have kept a glass back. Drinking from the bottle was a dangerous habit. It could be an indulgence just this once, though.

She turned to the pit, tilting her chin in an empty challenge, before she sipped more wine and put the bottle down. Turning to the bathroom, she nipped in, grabbing a towel – all fresh again.

Returning to the light, she stripped beside the bath, eyes hovering on the pit. Loosening her bra last, she wrinkled her nose at it as she set it atop the folded clothes. Probably no need to wear one in here, but she still dressed like she would leave. Because she would. Somehow.

Shaking herself a little, she dipped a hand into the water, waggling her fingers to make the bubbles swirl. She gripped both sides of the tub and stepped in, letting herself sink down.

Her skin flared in protest, a rush of heat singing along her blood, but she liked the water hot and if there was a tide line of red against her skin that was no different to home.

Home.

Home brought memories of Jenny, how she would tease Stephanie for her baths. How she would make her add cooler water to avoid any fainting spells after one incident. The way the cats yowled at the bathroom door if she closed it and Jenny was out, like they had been abandoned.

The memory stung more than the heat, and she took a shaky gulp, dunking herself under the surface to shock the tears away. She stayed there, her breath slipping out in silver bubbles that rose like stones skimming the surface of a pond, hounded by the thump of her pulse in her ears. Holding her breath wasn't a problem, so she lay in the too-hot water until the tingling under her skin died down.

Pushing back up, she breathed deep, savouring the burning in her lungs. Would drowning be possible? The room had limited her options.

Maybe she could smash a glass, or bend one of the metal straws in the fridge into a point, use that to slit her wrists. Didn't seem likely to take, given everything else, but blood had been a common theme. People bled quicker in the heat; that's why bathtub suicides were so popular.

She slid around onto her front, propping herself up so she could look over the lip of the tub. The dip of the pit was visible, though she was too low down to see into the darkness.

"What even are you?" She blew the bubbles away and let her chin rest on the side. "Not that I want you to answer."

She held her breath just in case, sighing when no response came. The water was cooling now, and she felt the air in sharp relief across her back, the earlier warmth stolen away. She would have to get out at some point, wrap herself in the large towel, and drying off by the fire made as much sense as anything.

Something in the air changed, the hairs on the back of her neck pulling up in a wave. Stephanie inspected the room. Nothing was different. The music still played. No whispering.

There was a smell, though. She'd grown used to the scent of the bathwater and the fire glowing away at the other wall, but something new crept in. It was acrid: out of place amongst the peat and perfume. She flipped back over, sitting up and grabbing the towel as footsteps echoed down the corridor.

Hopping out of the bath, sloughing water over the floor, she wrapped herself up. Heading to the fire to grab the poker, she caught flickering at the doorway. It was coming closer, approaching the room like someone carrying a candle, and growing brighter with the advancing sound.

She grabbed the poker and swung it behind her, one arm tucked around her hip, so it ran along her spine. It wasn't as warm as last night, but the weight in her hand was reassuring.

The footsteps were unhurried, someone drawing the journey out with no fear of being heard. Stephanie shrank back as the light expanded, the smell overwhelming when it pushed into the room as a herald.

It crested the corner, and for a moment she couldn't process what stood there. It was taller than her, an upright figure draped in heavy red cloth, the body hunched forward but still impossibly large, filling the entrance. Flames licked over the material—bright and hungry. The shape took a step inside, shedding small arcs of fire. The movement was slow, heavy, as if it ached to lift each foot.

A hood obscured whatever was under the blazing cloak. She was grateful.

There was no sound other than the crackle of flames, the music lost into the void of her and the room, the pit, this *thing* on fire.

It took another step, the shape under the hood lolling forward. The blaze drooped with it, splashing light across a flash of bone-white, then dropping into sparks.

Stephanie swallowed, stepping closer to the bath, so she had water nearby—the back of her head screamed that water would be better than that covetous fire. The creature crept on, slow progress punctuated with bursts of falling flame, until it stood across from her at the edge of the stone steps.

Then it looked at her, straightening up to full height and shaking the hood down. What should have been a face was a structured blur: a thick, fleshy space where eyes would fit, the gaping hole of a mouth. She felt the promise of the teeth, jumbled and sharp, a threat ghosting against her throat. Branching antlers creaked as the material slipped away, now alight themselves, wicked points going shiny with heat.

She screamed, and it mimicked her, the gap-mouth elongating into a chasm of points as flames soared up, encompassing it. When her voice cracked it stopped too, tilting its head softly before it pushed off the edge of the worked stone and hurled itself into the pit.

Something scraped against the edge and then light narrowed then dimmed as it tumbled down into the dark.

CHAPTER 9

Lunging for her clothes, she dropped her poker, the clanging loud in her ears as the music swelled into return. A slow violin piece. The notes dragged against her as she shoved legs into leggings, hands shaking as she forced her bra and top on in quick succession. She wanted the bar back. To unsee whatever that was, strike it from her mind with clear spirits.

Grabbing the metal bar, she abandoned the bath and went towards the bed, dipping to grab the book of plays. She would take that with her when she ventured down to get the bar back, an anchor in the storm. The music dimmed again. She stopped, chest constricting as footsteps began.

Shivering, she took the book and scrambled back to the bath, setting the plays on the floor beside the spilled water. It was a good vantage point for the door and corridor, kept her away from whatever this was without having to be in the bathroom. Folding down she went to one knee, bowing her shoulders to get full cover from the bath. She hugged the poker close across her chest, metal pressing insistently against her hip.

The light crept in as the footsteps advanced, shadows jerking erratically across the floor. Each step was heaved like they carried an immense weight. She heard it come round the corner, saw drips of flame sloughing off.

Leaning lower, she tipped her head to look around the side of the bath.

It was identical: a tall, hunched shape that littered fire. From here she saw the cloth was red velvet, thick as the curtains throughout the hotel. It draped over the creature head to foot, the bare impression of thin legs swamped by flames.

She ducked behind the bath and waited; breath trapped in her throat. Her eyes watered from the smell, like burning hair and flesh. The footsteps had stopped. There was just her own frantic heart and the crackle of two fires.

A grunt interrupted the stretching silence, starling her. The poker fell from her grip and she shot up, grabbing it as she went, bringing it up around the back of her head like a batter ready to swing.

The creature had thrown off its hood, flaming antlers shaking as it looked back and forth for her. She stared at it, glaring as it fixed what should have been eyes on her, the maw of teeth stretching into a near smile.

It leant closer, the material hissing like dry leaves in the wind. She swallowed, shaking her head, any words she could form dying on her lips. It was waiting for something, peering at her.

"G-go away," she whispered, voice small in her arid throat. It gave a little shudder, then screamed, the sound of tearing metal or breaking rock. She jolted back, kicking the book.

The creature nodded to her, once, then flung itself into the pit.

The light disappeared swiftly with its drop.

The poker wobbled dangerously near her head—she dropped her arms and hugged it to her chest. The shaking would stop. It could only last while the adrenaline was pumping.

The music came back while she was whispering herself calm, the same dirge-like violin notes. Maybe it was mourning those creatures, lost into the pit. The idea made a thrill of manic laughter bubble from her, alien in her ears.

The bed loomed close by, the solace of unconsciousness a siren to her aching mind. Would they find her under the covers? It felt childish, but it had worked last night.

Her indecision caught her out as the music slowed, then dipped again, heavy footprints starting anew. They boomed down the corridor, loud enough to send her shoulders up around her ears.

The stench was powerful enough to make her retch, not just flesh and hair but the haunting caress of rot. *Sickness*. It smelled like someone was burning down a hospital, or a plague pit, a miasma of disease surrounding her like gundogs on a hunt. She gripped the edge of the tub, poker by her leg, kneeling so just her head peered over the lip.

Fire licked along the corridor ceiling, leering closer as it spread into the room, the approaching steps singing through her bones. The smell was so bad she had to breathe through her mouth.

It was as broad as the doorway, this creature, the heralding flames pouring out of the cowl hood like a furnace. This fire was a furious blue, the swirls of a distant galaxy in the darker nights, and the heat surged off as it loomed closer, tipping forward to support itself on two broad fists against the floor. She guessed it was swathed in red velvet but the flames made it indistinct, too bright to tell.

With a thunderous growl, it shook the hood away, rocking forward on its knuckles. The antlers stretched impossibly up and out, a jagged splay of thorny points that scraped the ceiling. The fire ran through them with a hungry certainty, caressing the torn plaster.

She wasn't sure when she started to scream but it must have been the face—sharp angled, pale as a corpse in the flickering light. It had eyes, round and luminous yellow like burning coals. The teeth took up so much of the pointed jaw they seemed to overspill, curling out past the chin to disappear into flames.

One huge hand lunged forward, curling over the lip of the sandstone. Scaled fingers splayed out, gripping until the stone split and shards dropped towards the pit. It roared—the sound of waves crashing a boat into pieces. Of her mind shaking free from fear and rushing blindly into the will to flee.

Grabbing the poker, she twisted her body towards the bathroom corridor, her eyes on the monster in front. The cramped space was too small for it to fit: the antlers and mountainous shoulders too huge.

She bobbed on her feet, surging forward and pulling against the tub to give her momentum. Her feet twisted, the tepid bathwater making her legs fly out underneath her weight, and she went down. She sprawled onto her chest, yelping as her face bounced off the floor. Her vision swam and she gripped her head against the pain, her pulse loud over the bellowing creature. Blood flooded her nose, hot as the fire, and she had no time left to run.

With a sickening crash it threw itself over the pit and leaned around the tub, eyes sweeping like a lighthouse beam. She curled in on herself, twisting under the bath. The pit lurked on her right, open and inviting as the creature's claws raked through the air beside her arm. Stifling a whimper with one hand, she glanced around for the poker, lost in her fumbling. It sat off to the left—the creature must have knocked it away. The book of plays was beside her, though. She stretched to the side and grabbed it, white knuckled as she gripped it across her hips. The weight wasn't much, but she could swing it at this angle and stay in cover, bat claws away.

The creature stomped around the open area, broad head swinging as it sniffed and tore up the room. The flames spun off it, tumbling in clumsy arcs that hissed into nothingness.

Something chuckled, a tinkling sound like glass breaking. Stephanie froze, swallowing hard against the sob in her throat, her eyes screwed shut. Turning her head, she opened her right eye, peeking towards the pit. At the edge of the steps, less than an arm's length away, the face from last night was staring at her.

The golden eyes and lips were sparkling, merry at the wreckage from the creature's flailing. There was no skin, just the translucent impression of a shape, thin and oval, and the claws resting on the sandstone. It rapped them against the glittering ledge, loud against the backdrop of destruction. Stephanie shook her head. The face smiled wider, drumming the stone again.

The creature swung its head, jaw lolling open as it peered about. The whispering from the pit began again as the monster stomped closer. Stephanie gasped when thin claws caressed her right shoulder, just shy of piercing the skin.

She shuffled away from the pit, willing her body to be smaller, shrink beneath the bath so she could disappear through the dark plughole. The face blinked and laughed, sinking lower so just its eyes could be seen. A high-pitched scream broke Stephanie's focus, the creature beside her and scrabbling for purchase against the edge of the tub. A clawed finger found her hip, piercing through the book of plays to lance into her flesh, yanking her out from under the bath.

Her scream was an animal sound, the claw grinding again her hipbone. It let go; the book bouncing down onto her wound and she howled again, nauseous and furiously afraid.

She flipped herself over, hiding her wound, one hand slick with blood. The edge of the book was propping her hip up, giving her purchase but aggravating the skin. Grabbing it in her free hand, the other pressed to her wound, she turned over again, meeting the face of the creature as it leaned close to sniff her, sulphurous eyes unseeing. Shrieking, she grabbed the book in both hands, beating at the yellow orbs as hard as she could.

It reared back, flaring its claws, and she rolled towards the poker, stretching her arm out. Warm metal met her hand, and she clutched it to her, throwing it up against the claws. The poker skewed the creature's angle off enough that it only snagged her injured hip, the knotted pain making her head swim.

She kicked against the floor, the creature, anything to get away. The fire licked against her skin, stinging like a bite as it went over her bare foot, melting her leggings into a warped cast against her leg. Screaming at the pain, she dragged her legs closer, making it onto her knees. An acrid smell of fused plastic crept above the stench of disease, chemically contrasting, clinging to her woozy fury. The giant head of the creature was level with her own, the antlers scoring burning holes into the walls as it struggled to stand.

Stephanie forced herself up, careful to avoid the blood daubed across the floor, leaning against the wall. Cocking one leg up, she pressed her foot into the warm stone for purchase, angling herself forward. Launching off the heated stone she lunged her body weight into the side of the monstrosity, back turned to protect her face from the fire.

It lurched, bellowing, and she brought the poker up to capture the base of the antlers, locking her arms so she could wrench the face—and fire—away from her. Leaning her weight in, she pushed her hips back against the wall, grunting as blood leaked across her abdomen. Pain sang through her, but she ground her teeth, tensing her stomach. The heat was quick in her lungs, air too thin, her hands throbbing with burns from her grip.

Arcing her back, she drove forward, angling the monster towards the bath. It reared, almost upsetting her footing as the antlers scored tracks through the ceiling. She planted a foot to the join of the wall and shouted as she forced its head over the lip of the bath. Grunting, she tipped fully forward, the fire luridly dancing over her skin as she dropped her weight, pushing the face into the water. The creature thrashed, antlers knocking into her, but they were just a brushing burn, nothing in response to the molten pain of her hip, the knife edge of heat against her palms.

There was a hacking sound as the fire changed from blue to vibrant yellow, then to bloody red, the animal shuddering against her.

The fire stuttered out.

She bit the inside her lip, tensed, before the creature seemed to shatter, body going lax and sloughing apart. The antlers dropped away from her, the loss of the counterweight sending her towards the scalding water together with the bulky head. She squeaked, throwing her hands up to catch the edge of the bath. The poker dropped into the water like a stone thrown in on winter's day.

Untangling herself from the edge, she tested the water with her hand, yanking back at the burn. She let herself step backwards, backwards, until she bumped into the wall. It was rough against her back, and shards of stone were littered about the floor like scattered leaves. Something poked into her muscle like a talon. She had to get to the bar, get something to wash out the hole in her that beat a drumline of pain in time with her pulse.

First, the poker. She could pour the water out. Tip it down the damn pit, drown that smirking face. She settled for pulling the chain, watching the blackened water swirl away, the flakes of rotten flesh coalescing at the plug like birds fighting at a feeder. The poker was sitting across the warped skull, the bumps of where the antlers had connected snagging it.

Tugging one of her sleeves down, she grabbed the metal, tossing it towards the bed. One thing down. She shuddered, breathing open-mouthed and regretting the choice as the wet fug of the remains crept over her tongue. Heaving, she turned away, wheezing against the urge to vomit and grasping her side so she'd focus on the quicksilver pain instead.

Spirits would work for cleaning. Anaesthetic and antiseptic all in one, the gift that kept giving. The room spun around her for a moment and she moved towards the bed, willing her legs to get close enough that a fall would not damager her. She stumbled to the foot of it, grateful when her shins brushed against the covers.

Tipping forward, she splayed her hands out, supporting her weight, sank one knee onto the edge. She could do this. Crawling onto the mattress, she snagged a pillow, wrapping the poker in it folded length ways, hugging it. The heat was still here, but less.

Shuffling towards the edge of the bed, she went to stand, freezing when the same crystal laughter as earlier echoed through the room. The face was at the threshold of the pit, what would have been a chin now propped up on one set of claws. It smiled at her, glancing to the tub. The golden eyes blinked, gave the impression of raising, but she didn't know how they did that, how she could feel them doing it when there was no face.

Pushing up, Stephanie hugged the hot pillow-poker to her bleeding side, then walked back towards the bath. Weaving a little on her feet, she soon located the maimed book of plays, burnt edges smouldering. She bent to pick it up, hissing against the popping sensation that brought to her wound, and grabbed the open cover.

Walking back towards the door, she tossed the book at the pit, not looking to see if it hit the face.

CHAPTER 10

- -

The corridor was a cooling oven, the scorch marks stretching in shadowy branches. Stephanie traced their path along the ceiling, stomach tightening at the buildup of residue at the door. Limping closer, she ignored the fact that the paintings had changed, were now windows into disaster: ships on fire, cities burning down to the riverfront.

Leaning against the door, the buttons bled together before her eyes. The music option had popped out at some point and she laughed, hugging the pillow tighter.

Gulping air, she put her hand onto the wall beside the shiny buttons, the little orbs watching her. She poked the *bar* choice viciously. The glow from her room faded, then returned, the heavy sound of material dragging. Her head dropped to the side, resting against the door for a beat while she prepared for what was next. The cool glass was firm against her aching skull and she let a slow breath out, her gaze on the metal vines.

The temptation of opening the door to scream at Thomas occurred, but a wave of nausea broke her concentration. She gripped her weapon closer, pushing herself away.

Staggering along the corridor, she only had to pause twice, right arm braced up against the wall to support her weight. She kept her eyes on the floor—refused to meet any of the dead-eyed stares glaring at her—as she panted through the pain.

Gin. Vodka would do if she had trouble with the bar optic, but gin was what she needed, the navy strength stuff that would burn worse than the flames, but it would be a good burn. Clean. Fuck dying of septicaemia in this rotten place.

Rounding into the room the bar awaited her, the optics lit in the evening's gloom. The space was pristine once more—no sign of the chaos the monster gouged out—the bath mercifully absent. She should have tugged the skull out, kept it as a trophy. A flash of its unseeing eyes crept across her mind and she shook the image away, seeking liquid salvation.

Laying the poker and pillow across the bar, she turned to the row of clear spirits and selected the gin. Flipping it out of confinement, she plucked the spirit measure from the neck and poured two fingers into a glass, then grabbed some cranberry juice. Better to give her body sugar. The army spoke about that on nights out: keeping the hangover at bay with mixers and fruit juice.

The wound was tacky, the tug of material dried into the crusted blood snatching gasps from her when she leant forward. She knew the procedure for this—though she'd never needed to do it to herself. It was still in her head with the rest of her service training, kept tucked away to avoid unsettling other memories with longer shadows.

She gripped the glass, chugging the drink back in a couple of long gulps. Pouring another, she topped it up with cranberry juice again, adding a splash of orange so it didn't seem so shockingly red. There was enough red.

Twisting on her feet she leaned against the bar so her hips pushed forward, crying out when the material tore free of scabs. Pulling on her waistband she shimmied it down to sit on the cusp of her pelvic mound, shivering at the exposure. It was worse than being naked in the bath—more vulnerable, somehow.

"We can do this." The words sounded hollow. She gripped the bottle but hesitated, turning slightly so she could tug the pillow out from under the poker. It was oven-warm and fusty, the scent of hot metal too close to blood. She drizzled a little gin over the corner she held closest, then set it between her teeth and took a deep breath. Juniper filled her nostrils and the liquid burned pleasantly.

She focused on that feeling, teasing her tongue along the threads as she set the bottle against her heated skin. The glass was unyielding against the pain. She took a couple more huffs, gritting her teeth before she tipped the bottle.

The sudden contrast of icy liquid and then quick, flaring pain was enough to make her gag, the pillow almost slipping free. She grabbed it, folding her arm into her chest. Sucking harder on the corner, she tipped the bottle again, dribbling the gin over the wound like she was decorating a caramel coffee for Jenny. Jenny liked them on lazy Sunday mornings. Focus.

It was like being torn into anew, making her sweat and groan, pain seething at the edges of her.

Pulling the bottle away, she peered over the pillow. Her skin was pale and damp, the dried blood flaking away and running towards her leg in raspberry pink. She should have cleared more material away, really.

Setting the bottle down, she gulped more of her drink, holding the last mouthful until it warmed against her tongue. Delaying the inevitable.

She set the glass down, leaning into the bar and taking the pillow in her mouth again. This time she got a good grip with her teeth, gritting them before she grabbed the bottle. Two more washes should do.

Tipping the bottle, she pressed it into her skin, letting the alcohol leak out like she was dabbing perfume. The pressure above her wound was a dull insistence against the sharp alcohol, but it was easier to keep it there and let the liquid seep. She counted to ten, pulling the bottle away to check the wound. It was leaking fresh crimson at the bottom, but that meant the cleaning was working, pushing out any putrid remains.

There was a bar cloth somewhere, a small towel she could dab at the edges with. Glancing about she found it tucked into the gap between the little fridge and the counter, tugging it out. Her wound grumbled, but held.

The towel looked scratchy, but the fuzzy warmth of the alcohol would help with that, so she pushed it cautiously against her skin, dabbing around the wound and wiping out towards the floor. It was mostly a puncture, a dark hole in her that would swallow her up if she peered too closely. There was some tearing to the lower part where she'd been dragged, but it was minimal. Much as she hesitated to say it was lucky, the memory of those pushing teeth made her retch.

Steeling herself for one more go, she let her jaw relax for a moment, holding the pillow. She would dress the wound after this; cover it so she could lie down and contemplate how much she hated this place.

Taking the cotton back between her teeth, she pressed the bottle close, the fluid splashing out with her shaking. It was fine; would have to be fine because she sure as hell couldn't do this again. The gin seeped over her hip, spreading out like a grasping hand and she shuddered, pillow dropping from her mouth as she cried out.

"Fucking hell!" She didn't know who she was shouting at: the pit, herself, the dead creature.

She pulled the bottle away, plonking it on the counter with a defeated sob. Her whole abdomen was cold and throbbing - pain pulling everything taught. Kicking the pillow away, she grabbed her drink, draining it before setting the glass down, carefully. No glass shards today. No more ways to slice parts open. Peering over to the pit, she weighted the glass in her hand for a beat but set it back down.

Folding the bar cloth into a square she wiped it around the mouth of the bottle, letting it soak up the gin. Pressing this into her wound, she picked up the poker in her free hand, limping to the bed. Her steps were slow, and each swing of her left leg tugged distantly, but the alcohol had given her enough buzz to be separate from it: to make her pain inconvenient rather than inconsolable.

The pit face popped up as she reached the bed, peering at her from the steps. It tilted to one side, the eyes almost vertical to one another, the lips splayed wide in a shark's grin.

"Like the smell of blood?" She spat the question, sitting down in a slow manoeuvre. Pushing her hand against the wound, keeping her fingers spread against the edges in as close to an even pressure as she could manage, it made the pain less invasive. She kept the poker close, the handle at her thigh.

Her case was still tucked beside the bed and she tugged it closer, tipping it onto its back. Pulling the zipper around was an exercise in patience, having to pause every few centimetres to sit up and let the chasing pain abate, but she finally shoved the top free.

Plain beige tights sat nestled into the mesh compartment. Leaning closer, she tugged it open just enough to slip her hand inside and grab them, fingers circling around them as if they were a life buoy.

She didn't bother to close the case as she fell back, bringing her legs up with her. A small cry pulled out, even the drunk haze not enough to make that pain fade off. So sharp. So hungry. Doing this laid down must be easier.

Planting her feet against the frame, she pulled the tights underneath her, setting the crotch close to her wound and pulling a leg across her stomach. These were a good brand—she could probably make them loop over. Screwing her eyes shut, she pulled them tight against her wound, crossing them over at the opposite hip. The pressure was not agony, a welcome reprieve, though maybe that was the booze. Whatever the cause, she was grateful.

She clenched her lower stomach, keeping the muscles taut as she pushed her hips up. It sent a jolt of pain through her and she dropped onto the bed, tears flaring hot and thick, blinding her. She paused, sobbing open mouthed against the aftershocks as she tensed again. Nearly there. She needed the leg in her right hand underneath her and over to the left side. Then she'd tie the legs together, tuck the knot into the waistband. That would be out of the way, unlikely to snag in the night.

Gritting her teeth, she pushed up again, lifting only her right side so she could tuck her hand as far under her hip as possible. Trembling, she sank back down, letting her head fall. Reaching around with her left hand, she rocked to her right, grunting against the tug on her shoulder and clutching until her fingers met. Sagging, she grasped the other tights leg in her right hand, breathing out slowly as she tightened the binding.

The pressure over her abdomen was enough to make her nauseous but she could push against that, use the background burn of too much gin and juice, too much *fuzz,* to be sure of her actions. It would be enough. It had to be.

With a slow focus she tied the tights together, doubling the knot before she curled the waistband around it. It was enough to hold for the night. She would take the gentle press of this instead of the open agony of ruptured skin.

Sitting up, she grasped the poker. It sat on the bedspread like a broom handle, some old promise of lines not to be crossed. She laughed: this suite was a testament to boundaries broken. Sighing as she lowered down onto her back, she pulled the cover over on itself, cocooning herself into the half-formed shape. It wasn't as safe as last night, but she had the cover, and her poker, and exhaustion was chasing through her blood just as quick as the alcohol.

CHAPTER 11

- -

S leep rolled across her in shallow waves, punctuated by gull-cry sobs against the pain. Each stretch or turn brought a lancing reminder, left her in the fleeting, untethered space behind her eyelids. The duvet was a soft layer of surf, obscuring anything in the surrounding depths: a comfort as much as a bind.

It wasn't that she woke up with fright. Rather, the adrenaline pushed through what little rest she grasped, left her panting. She batted the material, finding a corner to peel away and gulp cool air.

Her whole hip ached, but it was better than the biting agony last night. She curled onto her side, and half into herself, bring her knees close so she could roll into sitting. The expected pain didn't come, though it shot through her when she stood; the bolt enough to make her sit, moans lost to the blood rushing in her through her ears.

Pressing a hand against the wall, she tried again, carefully stretching. The pain slithered along her like a hungry snake, but she could push it aside, make it a detached part of her mind, instead of the overwhelming scream.

Looking over at the bar, she contemplated more gin. There was no food, no indulgence in a sandwich or cake. Or a fry up. The warmth and distance alcohol would give was a yearning deep in her chest, but she picked up the poker and shuffled towards the doorway, peering around before she limped along the corridor.

The paintings were the same—fire and death, accusatory eyes demanding she witness the destruction. The scorch marks still littered the ceiling like a giant charcoal mistake, some impressionist's whim of a nightmare. She kept her gaze on the shiny white tiles below her and then on the door at the end, the metal vines that beckoned her closer.

Her steps were slower today, the delay a mix of pain and anxiety. She could have used the poker as a cane, if she trusted her weight against the tip, but between the pointed risk and the slick shine of the tile, it was just more pain begging to be realised. She set it underneath the list of buttons, leaning it into the corner so it was handy.

The cool glass greeted her like a frozen pool, marvellous on her skin. Maybe she had an infection. She didn't want to know. That was a problem for later. Leaning into it, she let her breath fog up the panel, watching the faux frost mirror the coating on the other side. She could almost imagine Thomas watching her from his spot in the centre of the floor—a conductor in the maelstrom of the dead—enjoying her paltry impact on the suite.

She opened the door, stepping out and setting her heel against the bottom of the wood to keep it open. It wouldn't lock her out. She didn't like her chances of moving quickly, though, and doing this meant the weight was off her injured side. Her arms crossed automatically, some small defiance against the absurdity.

The buzz of activity sprang into action: the crowd of greyed shapes swarming into unlife, the hall erupting in creeping mould like a stained-glass window of corruption. The growl of the ever-hungry void began.

Thomas was looking at her with the prudish revulsion of someone unsettled in church: a mix between a sneer and a grimace. His lips were darker than before, almost blue, and his eyes had sunk in.

"You look like shit," she said.

"You murdered a member of the hotel."

Her eyebrows swooped up, a bark of surprise spilling out. "Oh, were they guests?"

"Valued colleagues."

"I'd hate to see the Christmas parties."

"Do you think this pantomime of resistance will get you anything?" Dark blood sprayed from his mouth.

She took a dull, blossoming satisfaction at the idea she was hurting him. It was probably the cost to the hotel, the strain he'd spoken about before. It had been days. What was the point of days here? The murky light from the windows let her know time had passed, but time was different here, he told her that, so maybe it had been years. She was tired enough for it to have been that long. Her injury, her pain, that was new, as was his degrading mania—those would be in her memory if they weren't new.

The rumble of the void rattled closer, shaking her attention back, the top of the nearby steps blinking into darkness. "It seems to piss you off."

"Only in the inelegance. You're murderous. And injured."

"Correct."

"The hotel could remedy that for you, rather than you succumbing to blood poisoning. You'll rot, you know. Everything does here." He held his hand up with a flourish, extending his fingers and circling them to indicate the ecosystem seeping across the walls.

"Would I be one of those whispering voices in the pit?"

"If you simply die in there, your body will be recycled, and your belongings consumed. You gain nothing. No one will know where your bones lie, no one will mourn you, you'll just be someone else that went missing in the city." He brushed imaginary threads from his shirt, as if it weren't stained and bloody, holes left from his terminal ministrations.

She bristled at his tone: haughty. Dismissive. She wanted to sink her fingers into those sharp, stupid eyes. "Did no one miss *you*? I have a girlfriend. Friends. People will know I'm gone."

"They might. And that grief will do them as much good as it did you. At least if you join the hotel, you could be part of something, but the longer you linger the harder it will be. Don't you want to be something more?"

"Fuck you." She stepped towards him, but pain flourished anew over her side, the movement switching her weight without thinking. She gasped, her hand going to her side on reflex, glowering at him as he smirked back.

"How long do you think you'll cope with that, untreated? Until a fever, or until it starts to smell? You'll be crawling into the pit."

The void crunched heavily, steps gone, the tiles of the hall fraying at the edges like an unloved carpet. She leant back against the wood and glass, sagging. "Are painkillers part of the room service? I can't see a button for them."

"There's plenty of alcohol."

"How'd that work for your wounds?"

He laughed, a guttural sound like a clogged drain. "I'm looking forward to working with you, once you're part of us."

She chewed her lip, leaning back into the door to slip away. The poker was still waiting for her underneath the buttons, cool. She drooped against the door, the echoing sound of the void gone, just her own unsteady breathing. Letting her head loll to one side, she contemplated the buttons. She still had the bar. The seat. The windows. She pushed the button for music and limped back to the room.

The art had changed. Instead of the destructions from earlier now she had crowds, swelling scenes of people watching executions or battles, canvases that oozed red. One was a man having his head cut off by two struggling women, their layered, draping dresses making her think it could be a biblical scene. Next to it, in another painting, a grinning demon peered over the scene of one man wrestling another, ripping his opponent's throat out with his teeth.

She hesitated at a statuette presented on a new squat table, a rough impression of two figures, one splayed out and the other leaning over to cradle the first's head in its lap. There was just the barest impression of colour over the white glazed pottery. The one prone had a wash of red around its head, the kneeling one with drips of blue running down what could have been a face.

It brought an aching that pushed through the pain of her wound to bring her to tears. Swallowing against the lump in her throat, she turned away from it, limping away.

CHAPTER 12

- -

H er accompaniment today was a slow waltz, picking up as she entered the suite. It was once again neat and ready: bed made, fire stacked. Gripping the poker tighter, she went to the bar in dragging steps, around the seat and past the unlit fireplace. Drinking the pain away was an option, and one that had served her well so far, but the heat in her blood was just as likely to be incandescence as infection.

Thomas's words looped around her skull, taunting her about Jenny. Like he knew her girlfriend, or their love. Their sacrifices. Like he could even remember being human! She'd given up the army for Jenny—had little choice once the military police had found evidence of them being together, despite their being so careful. Jenny wouldn't just forget her.

Thomas didn't know anything. He was just a walking corpse leaking bits of red.

Maybe he'd been here a long time. Long enough that ice picks were normal in hotel rooms when he died. Had that ever been the case in Glasgow? There had been gang wars historically—razors and ice cream—young men slicing each other into pieces. A pick was less use for that, realistically, but it could still kill someone. Evidently.

She shook the thought off, reaching the bar and leaning in. Her wound throbbed, beating with her pulse, and the urge to peel back the makeshift dressing was a deep itch under her skin.

Sighing before she pushed up, she shuffled around to the other side, grasping the gin bottle and bringing it down from the optic. Setting the poker on the bar behind her, she hissed air at the twang of pain that cost, the tug of something stretching a little too far. There was no sudden heat, no tang of iron in the air, and that was a mercy cheap enough to match the gin.

Setting her back against the bar, she turned the waistband of her leggings down, folding them over themselves a few times. The tights were still there; a little askew but holding. She slipped a finger under the elasticated material at each hip, skin itching in the cool air. Easing the stretched loop away, she saw a smattering of deeper red on the bar cloth, but it was just a Rorschach shape—not the spreading stain of new bleeding.

She peeled the folded square from her hip, material damp with her sweat but mostly clean. There was the smell of old blood, but none of the lingering sickness of the beasts. No rot. The cloth slipped through her fingers, shape loosening now it wasn't compressed. It didn't fall, though, the crust of dry blood holding fast.

This was going to hurt.

Taking the bottle, she tugged the optic measure out, dropping it on the counter, tightening and loosening her grip on the glass twice before she lifted it. She had to check the wound, make sure there was nothing coming out of it but blood. Then she could put a fresh cloth on it and wrap it.

Huffing a quick couple of breaths, she tipped the gin bottle towards her abdomen, pressing it tight against the skin so the slightest amount dribbled out. She clenched everything she could, stomach tight, ignoring the way it pulled the wound higher and made her teeth grind. Shifting the bottle down she let it rest a little above the cloth, panting at the effort to keep everything tight. Her brow was wet, the hot smear of sweat spreading up the back of her neck and across her shoulders.

Tilting the neck towards her chest, she let some of the gin leak down in trickles, holding her breath against the sting. She had to suck air in once it made contact, the cold shock of the fluid quickly replaced by vicious heat, letting her peel the cloth away in a gradual line that revealed a milky layer of dead cells in the centre.

Her head fell back as the cloth finally came free, and she let the wound air for a moment, eyes shut as she struggled to keep still. There was more to do, more pain to follow: she had to dress it again. The glass of the bottle pushed against her hipbone, the promise of more fire for her wound, and she felt one knuckle pop as she tightened her grip.

Opening her eyes, she brought the cloth up to squint at it, the layers of colour not meaning much anymore beyond DIY injuries when she and Jenny went through a crafty phase. The thought of Jenny made her hiccup round a sob and she bit into her lower lip, looking around the room. She wanted to see her photo, look at the two of them together on her phone screen. Her case was still beside the bed, she could do that when this was finished, could lie down and cradle the useless lump of technology between her hands like it was Jenny's face.

The wobble of the bottle let a leak of gin out, and she flinched. The cloth in her hand was better than she'd expected, the dead cells a mix of white and creamy orange: more likely scabs than lingering infection. There was none of the yellow from those glowing eyes, no green like the walls outside the suite. Tossing it to one side she grabbed a new cloth, eyeing the container. Only one left after this. Three cloths was cheap. Perhaps it would refill overnight. She snorted at the idea, flopping the cloth against the countertop to fold a new square. It was smaller than the last, but it would still work as a dressing, something to keep the rot at bay.

Once she was happy with the shape, she put it below the bottle and let some gin soak the cotton. Hopefully it was cotton. Maybe that was part of the recycling, older items turned into new. She sniffed, head swimming. Her stomach had gone slack at some point, soft skin pushing against the bottle. When the cloth was nicely wet, she pulled the bottle away with shaky hands. It came off with a light slop, a dash of gin going across her thighs, but it was tolerable. She wouldn't notice it once she was drinking.

Standing straighter again, she peered at her hip, looking at the tear in her skin. The edges were stark white, more like office paper than the mellow bone colour she was expecting, and they were a little puckered, but it looked smaller than last night. That seemed alright. Nothing looked slimy, or smelled bad, not that she could get much other than gin. What she could see inside was an angry red, a reasonable colour between the blood, trauma, and compression. Red meant alive.

Rest was needed for a wound like this, staying in bed and not moving too much. Stitches, too. The room didn't have a sewing kit, and she hadn't packed a stapler, so that wasn't happening. She should have bought one of those stupid travel kits, a little casket the size of your thumb that carried needles and a bobbin of thread to sew a button back on. This was a bit more visceral, but those threads came with a guarantee.

She took a few deep breaths, getting her chest full of air and blowing it out in a hard, slow rhythm as she slapped the new square over the wound. The whole wound flared with pain, an aggressive push of stimulation she wasn't ready for, and she cried out as she ground her spine into the bar as an anchor, so her hand was pressing her into the cool stone. Her chest heaved, too little air in the room to quell the burning, to extinguish the sobs in her throat.

Her free hand scrabbled for the tights, trembling as she slipped two fingers underneath the stretchy material. She worked the loop higher in increments, afraid a quick tug would cause a ladder—or worse, a hole—which would invariably spiral into this becoming a useless endeavour. It took several choking breaths before the tights were in place, securing the cloth. It had been easier laid down.

The waistband was next, pulled away from her body as she brought it gingerly up to cover the dressing, the elastic biting as she slowly, slowly, settled it in place. She stood, simply breathing, for a few beats, her wound now back to a dull ache. The pain was less intimate now, swaddled under layers, but it pressed on her like a weight.

Leaning forward, she set her hands against the counter and spreading her fingers wide, bracing her weight against the cool top. It sent a shiver through her but nothing else and she shifted her weight across to the right, resting most on her arm while her left hand felt for the top of the fridge. It was easy to snag her fingers into the seam of the door, to pry it open with a couple of crooked knuckles dug in and clawing.

The rows of bottles stood waiting: green glass lined up like trees along the edge of a graveyard, the metal straws hemming them in as a makeshift fence. Fruit sat in a little tray at the front, a splash of red disturbing the dim space. A flash of life in the chill morgue of alcohol and metal. The image of the figurines in the hallway pushed forward, sad shapes looming large in her memory.

Dipping her arm so she could keep her core tight, she lowered closer to the fridge, feeling out one of the wines. Straightening her arm, she lifted the bottle with a grunt, just a brush of pain as she lifted. It came up and out of the fridge easily, thumping down on the counter next to the gin, a thinner, more indulgent companion to the bottle of spirit.

The door flopped closed with a fat slap and she let out a shaky breath, the sweat across her forehead leaking into her eyes. She wiped it away with her left hand, still propped up on the right, then started on the cork. If she had been thinking ahead, she would have taken a straw as well, to make lifting the bottle less effort later, but that was a problem for later. Now she just had to loosen the cork, and ignore the pain in her side until she could lie down and stare at Jenny's face. Yearn for her.

Taking the cork out required two hands, so she pulled up, testing her range of movement with a slow sway to each side. Moving to her right hurt, but it was tolerable, and shifting her weight to her left caused a burst of sharp, crushing pain, but it stopped when she pulled back. Keeping her weight on her right, she took the bottle in her left hand and worked the metal off with her right, gripping the cork and twisting with two quick grasps. It came off with a loud pop; the fizz rushing up the neck. She slurped the bubbles before they could spill over. The sugar made her tongue prickle, and she dropped the cork onto the counter. It bounced up at her but toppled over, semi-circling against its own weight for a few moments, and she contemplated flicking it away. Or throwing it into the pit.

The poker was still waiting for her on the bar when she turned, swapping the wine bottle into her left hand to take the poker in her right, heading towards the bed in steady steps. Her balance skewed to her right, away from the pain, the tug when she pulled her left leg forward making her abdomen ache by the time she reached the bed.

Her case was still there, the top set loosely over the larger compartment, and she flipped it open with the poker. The lid swung over with a soft thump against the floor, the items in the mesh segment skittering around. Her phone was there, making the black material sag with its weight.

Sitting down with a small grunt, Stephanie set the bottle of wine down on her far side, tugging the case closer with one heel, hand fishing for the phone. It took a few attempts, her hip straining with the effort to lean from her waist and not rise up on her thighs, but she grabbed it.

The screen flourished into life with a swell of light. She rocked backwards, bringing her knees up with her, and let herself tip onto the bed with the phone, rolling onto her right side once she was safe to do so. Shuffling up towards a pillow, she gingerly stretched her legs out, crooking her left knee to rest against the mattress and support her hip. Her breath caught in her chest, but she closed her eyes and made herself unwind, easing into the support. Once she had relaxed, she clicked the phone screen on again, smiling at the picture of her and Jenny—taken at some ridiculous winter market last year—and reached over to the bottle of wine, nestling it at the underside of her breasts so it didn't overbalance. It was a little precarious, but she kept her left hand loose on the glass, and stared at Jenny.

CHAPTER 13

- -

A t some point she fell asleep, because a wet slap against the ground brought her awake. Jerking up she fumbled—phone falling away into the case, the photo of her and Jenny vanishing—the bottle bumping into her and spilling body-warm wine. She flinched, sat up on the bed, sleep lingering over her longer than she liked.

Her hand went to her face, wiping tiredness and drink away. She couldn't see anything different—nothing sprawled out over the floor or loveseat. The music still played, a slow piano piece that was vaguely familiar.

Satisfied that nothing was out of place, she got up, carefully, nudging the case aside before she grabbed the poker and went to the pit. She hated the face now, fear a biting undertone to her anger. It didn't matter what it was, really; she had no time to imagine, didn't want to pollute her mind with wondering. She was well versed in keeping hold of her mind, locking nightmares and flashbacks away so they didn't overwhelm her new life. But she despised the facade of humanity the creature used:

blinking and giggling and acting like it had any resemblance to her. She would have done *much* worse if she had claws or those shiny, sharp teeth.

Once she was at the edge, poker held behind her to show she wasn't being aggressive, she peered over. The stones were clear, flecks of light reflecting off imperfections. The pit sat, dark and still, no whispering. No gold. She stepped back after a few beats.

She didn't want to go back down the corridor, and the music was still playing. Last night it had stopped with each creature, as if their pushing into the suite had disrupted something. It would be better if it were that, rather than just a warning—the hotel letting her know that doom was stalking her. Was it indulgent enough to give her warning? She didn't know which answer would be better.

Her shoulders sagged as she pressed herself into the wall beside the corridor, her poker tucked close. The metal was heavy against her thigh, an unyielding line reminding her she had some control. Not much, but this at least was a choice: better to know if something was down there. Settling her weight against the stone, she slipped her head around the corner, squinting as if it would help.

Nothing. The corridor was littered with art and smudged with soot across the ceiling. The music continued, unbothered by her. She pulled back, resting her shoulders against the wall, head bumping into the ridge between two of the large bricks. Notes washed over her in waves, tripping over the suspicion she held close as she took the room in again. Her fingers ached from gripping the poker.

She'd wash her face and then inspect the room. Just like packing up.

Going to the bathroom was slowed by a minor detour to the bed, collecting the discarded bottle, now near empty, and setting it on the bar.

Entering the bathroom she ignored the shower, fixed her eyes on her own reflection, refused to let anything other than the lights and her own shape creep in. Which was how she stepped in, and then leapt away from, a large red stain that had overflowed the shower and across the floor. She yelped as she stumbled back, one foot slick with what was almost certainly blood. It was *warm*. The sound from earlier came back to her, wet and heavy, and she looked to the shower to find splatters up the sides, a flecked pattern over the glass.

This was thick, not just the sticky viscosity of coagulation but half as deep as her thumb, with an uneven surface of clots. It didn't smell like blood in the room, none of the sharp tang she was accustomed to, but there was a dampness: mildew heavy in the air. She skirted around it, grabbing the stack of towels and wiping her foot off with a corner. Bundling the rest against her chest, she shuffled, tugging the door shut behind her.

She stared at the wood for a moment, as if it would rattle, or there would be more wet noises. The poker was up against her body, smothered by the towels, and she made herself turn away, back into the suite. Nothing was out of place. All that had changed was the bed being made, which meant she didn't need to wipe it down.

Nodding to herself, she went to the bar, setting the towels on the counter. She needed more wine. The fireplace was lit, but the poker was missing, probably because of being on top of her newly acquired stack of towels. The fire was usually an afternoon thing, if that had any meaning now. She'd slept a while.

She would drink wine to keep the pain off, then decide what to do next. No rush. Uncorking the wine with more enthusiasm than necessary, she took a few quick gulps, frowning against the scratching bubbles. She set the bottle down, opening the fridge again to look inside. A mixed drink wouldn't hurt. She could make something to sip, with a straw even, keep the open bottle until she relaxed enough that the sweet sharpness wouldn't bother her.

The optics were a catalogue of choices, so she clicked a glass under the gin twice, then added a vodka before she started picking fruit juices. Cranberry was a good option, red to match the warning of everything in this room, and tart enough to cut against the sugar. She picked up a metal straw as she pulled the juice from the fridge, stabbing it into a slice of lime for garnish, clinking it into the glass. Her side hurt, but it was still far enough away she didn't worry, planned to keep that distance through careful application of spirits and gentle movements. If she couldn't fix it, she could at least help it not worsen. It was almost rest.

Taking her poker and glass towards the bed, she laid the bar down against the mattress, turning to go back for the wine bottle. A flash of red caught her eye, darker than her juice. Blood seeped under the bathroom door, like a wave skimming towards the shore. Stark even against the wood. She stared at it for longer than she needed to, her eyes burning as she watched for movement.

It wasn't coming forward; it was just there. Bringing the glass up, she took two deep pulls through the straw, still watching it. She chewed her lower lip in thought, teasing the flesh between her teeth, aware this was the closest to food she had other than lime wedges and cherries. The thought made her laugh, an over-lubricated response. She needed the pleasant buzz, not to be drunk.

She took another quick suck, holding the drink in her mouth for a beat until it warmed, swallowing the tart combination. Drifting to the bar, she finished her glass, then took up the smaller towel she had wiped her foot with. Folding it in half lengthways twice, so it was a strip of four layers, she went back to the door and dropped it. Bending down was an increasingly bad idea, so she supported her weight on the doorjamb, moving the towel into the blood with her left, stained foot. Nudging until it was snug with the door, she tucked the corners in to the frame, edges lined up with the little gap at the bottom. Then she pressed it down in quick little stamps, so the blood didn't touch her.

Satisfied, she went back to the bar, raising the wine to her lips and swallowing a few mouthfuls. It would be better, now, the warmth created by the cocktail enough to stop pain from each sip, so the fizz was a sparkling irritant rather than a cruelty. She would need a fresh bottle shortly, certainly would need to grab some more before she went down the corridor, but taking a fresh bottle out before she had finished this seemed like too much of a crutch. Even if she could use one. Maybe she would mix another cocktail instead.

The bottle landed back on the counter with a loud clink, and she picked up the stack of towels, scooping them under her arm to sit against her waist. They might vanish with the bar if she pushed another button. There was no certainty in that, but what was certain in here, other than the pit? She took them over to the bed, dropping the stack onto the bedding to sit beside the poker. They bounced a little, tipping over to spill in an arc of cream cloth. Stephanie huffed at the movement, softly batting the towels back into a rough stack, mouth scrunched until they were back as they should be. She gave them a brief nod of approval and turned to go back to the bar.

More blood.

Chapter 14

The towel was soaked, bloody through the fabric and towards the wall, maybe an inch into the little stump hallway that led to the bathroom . Another towel needed. She picked a larger one from the pile, rearranging them to find a medium-sized bath sheet, folding it over itself.

That made a fat rectangle, as thick as her palm, and she went to lay it against the door. It covered the other towel, and the bigger stain, completely; rode up some of the height of the door too, so she pressed it in again with her foot. Nothing made it through the layers, and none of the blood seeped past the edge.

Now: wine. Retreating to the bar, she pulled a bottle out, then two more, because this seemed like an excellent memory to drown out. She lined them up on the counter, a little row, uncorking the one nearest and holding it to her chest. A hand covered her face reflexively, cloaking her eyes in darkness while she breathed through her nose and tried to control the trembling in her legs.

She was *fine*.

Lifting the bottle higher, she took a long drink, focusing on the hiss of bubbles. The music was still playing, but she'd lost focus, the instrument changing at some point. Now she had a cheerful waltz. It might be nice to listen to: sit on the bed and rest. She had to go back to the bed, and maybe take the bottles with her. Sitting down was a sudden necessity—the shaking in her legs too much.

The walk across was slow, but steady, bottle gripped tight in her left hand as she supported her weight against the bar with her right. Both were cool under her palm, but the glass warmed in her touch, a small yielding that made her smile. The poker awaited her at the edge of the bed and she moved it to the side, sitting between it and the remaining towels. It was almost company. She snorted and took another drink, turning to look at the towels.

"You come here oft—"

The towel against the door was soaked, even up to the folded crease, just the double-stitching still cream. She could have mistaken it for bleach marks on a red one, something discarded after a careless cleaner. The blood had continued past the material: the flow inching in a wide arc, reaching into the suite.

She shook her head, glancing quickly between the poker and the towels. She had two large ones left in the stack, bath sheets that would cover the others. They'd be as wide as her hand once folded, more than the creeping blood. There hadn't been this much in the stain from the shower. It had only been a couple of feet long, less than the height from her foot to her hip, maybe as broad as her forearm. Nothing sufficient to be oozing out this far. The suite was flat, too, no gradient for it to be pouring down.

Her hands found a towel, big enough to be worn around her like a dress. This was the second largest, coarser than the other two, more texture to grab and retain the insistent blood. Even her wound hadn't bled this much, and she'd been punctured. Clawed. The fuck did you call it when talons were involved?

She shoved the question away, stumbling up, still jittery, the towel half folded as she got closer. Then thrown down. She flicked it over itself with her foot, folding it again haphazardly in half, smothering the fluid. The towels underneath bunched together, bound by the blood, and she quickly bent at the waist to push the corners in, sealing the misshapen mess at the door. The bend cost her a shot of pain, but she swallowed against it, pacing backwards with a hand hovering at the ache. Nothing crept through, the smear of red from where she'd wiped the blood away just a bare wash of colour. Like the statuette in the corridor.

Pausing, she glanced over her shoulder, half tempted to go and get the statuette, compare the shades. It would mean bringing it into the room, but she could take a thing from the room into the corridor, so that should work. She turned back and screamed when she saw the new towel was sodden, red across with the determined puddle reaching closer.

"Fuck off, fuck off, fuck off!" She grabbed the last towel and came as close as she dared, going to her right knee to splay it across the short corridor, scooping the blood back towards the door. It was warm enough to be fresh, leaking through the material to press up against her palm in a wet kiss.

She gagged, flinching when one shove splashed blood up her wrist. She scrubbed her skin with the other hand, yanking a cream part of the towel up to wipe, scuttling away from the ruby streak eating closer.

Out of towels, she backed up to the bed, shoulders bumping the mattress. She tensed, unwilling to look away from the door, slapping her hand against the floor, the frame, eventually sinking her fingers into the duvet. She couldn't pull it one handed, not with her wound, but she could work her hand underneath the cover and get some air between it and the sheet.

Her fingers fumbled for the join of the spread, slipping too far and dropping to thump against the frame. The pain was sharp, bones in her knuckles and wrist throbbing with shock, and she glanced over before she could stop, checking for gore of her own.

"Shit!" She wasn't bleeding, but the towel was lost to the blood, tendrils of red now lancing towards her. It wasn't just trying to get into the room: they were reaching for her.

She grabbed a handful of the covers, leveraging against the weight to pull up and work her knees underneath herself, watching the blood. The poker slid about with her manoeuvring the cover, falling beside her with a loud clang that sent her shoulders up to her ears, the left one crunching internally, and she splayed her right hand out to find the metal, pull it close to her leg.

The duvet inched closer, enough that she could reach across to grasp it with both hands, plunging her fingers into the cotton. Hooking one knee up she got her right sole flat on the floor, tucking her weight so she could push up, core tight as she strained to keep her eyes on the door, wavering a little when her leg straightened. She put her left foot down. It hadn't moved more, the blood: it was still an uneven line of reaching, yearning shapes grasping towards her, and the duvet was king-size. It was warm, and soft, and made up of at least three layers with the cover on it too, and she would stamp that damn blood into it and shiver through the night if needed.

Dragging it free of the bed she held it in front of her like a shield, careful to keep watch on the door—the blood.

Taking a few shaky steps, she flicked the duvet so the end was closer to the tendrils of red, so no speck of blood was free. She stood on the edge, lowering the duvet down to cover most of the corridor. Blood did not immediately seep through, and she gingerly stepped into the edges, pressing her weight just enough to set the duvet flat before tottering back.

The music skipped a beat, hitching like someone at the instrument had been touched. Stephanie's heart lurched, unable to fight the instinctual turn, looking to the corridor lest the beasts of yesterday returned in fire and fury. Nothing shook. There was no beckoning rot, or rush of flames, but the panicked checking would cost her. She could hardly make herself turn back.

The duvet was heavy with blood that now pooled in the corners, rivulets stretching towards her. Jolting, she crept away from the movement, squeaking when her foot caught the poker and knocked it away. It rolled towards the pit, the scratch of metal against wood loud.

"Shit, no, shit!" She lunged for the poker, side flaring in pain, screaming in frustration when it reached the lip of the stone steps. The momentum made it tip over when it was a little past halfway across the edge, the handle flying up in an arc to tip itself over and down. She scrabbled after it, throwing herself onto the stone steps, hands outstretched to catch the poker, the metal glancing off the side of her palm and changing trajectory.

Her foot slipped, landing her down onto the layer where the pit waited, the open hole quiet. The poker turned over on itself again, the tip sweeping through the air as the handle bounced off the step and began to tumble into the darkness. She pitched forward, right arm thrown out for the etched stone at the far side, her left shoulder and head down the pit to grab the metal. Her hand closed around the pole and it rushed through her sweat-slick fingers, scratching her, but she gripped harder, the textured handle biting into her palm.

Clenching her fist until her fingers shook, she panted in the musty air of the pit, the chasm beckoning her for a long drop. All she could see was her hand and arm, the rest blank, and she tightened her abdomen as she pulled up, using her overtaxed right shoulder to work herself higher without straining the howling pain in her left hip.

Sweat drenched her, and she almost had herself out when a glint of gold shone in the dark depths. She shook her head, mouthing "no," and there was a sudden yank on the poker. It wasn't enough to wrench it from her, but it forced her back down, a cold kiss brushing her brow as the eyes were suddenly there, joyous, before letting go.

She sobbed as she shoved herself up, rearing away so her spine bumped into the steps. Nothing came after her, no claws or glittering eyes, but she could feel the lips, a stinging cold that her tears did nothing to dispel. She shuffled back, plonking her backside down on the higher stones and hugging the poker to her chest, pinching her eyes shut to force the tears out and clear her vision.

A smatter of warm fluid sprayed up the back of her neck.

Chapter 15

- -

M eaty air wafted across Stephanie as she put a hand to the wet patch on her neck, only half surprised when her fingers came back red. She stood up, turning to face what was in the bathroom corridor.

It was almost human shaped, had enough *parts* to be human. Two legs, but they were thicker at the bottom, with heavy stumps that seeped blood where it stood—splaying like a fungal spread. What may have been hips were wicked thin, tapering up into a slim torso with oversized shoulders, a pair of drooping, bottom heavy arms. Too many fingers in what served for hands, the joins gangly but the pads bulbous.

At the head was a nub, the round dome of a skull pushed out of the shoulders just enough to give the shape clarity, and coated in coagulating clots, lumpy areas that could have been hair or just thick rows of tissue. Where she would expect a face there were teeth, loose but in a rough line, and instead of eyes she saw floating, shifting shards of a mirror, catching the lights as they bobbed. Bits of silver seemed to glint all over the shape.

She could catch glimpses of herself in the shards, flashes of her own slack face, thinner than she had been and eyes a listless red from weeping.

It stepped into the suite, free from the duvet, pivoted towards her but not advancing. Stephanie shifted to the side, inching to her left so she could climb out. It did the same, tracking her movements.

A squelch accompanied each step, the lift of each stump a heaving, burdensome undertaking. The impacts spewed blood, a sweep of red that went across the room like arterial spray, painting her chest with gore. It was so warm—like the touch of someone else—like she'd been painted with before, when men were down and you had to rush to stabilise them. Her heart thudded at the memory, but she couldn't focus on it: she had to get herself onto the same level as whatever this was. At least have a chance of being on the same ground before it went for her.

Her calf bumped into the next level and she stilled, breath caught in her chest for a long moment, before she cautiously bent her knee and hovered it over the stone. The pain in her hip was there but less than it had been over the pit; she could move. It took a few deep breaths and tightening everything south of her diaphragm, but she forced her knee up with a grunt, foot slapping down against the gritty stone. She shuddered at the noise, but she could shift her weight slowly over to that leg now, eyes always on the bristling, squirming creature.

It teemed, almost advancing as it rocked forward but swayed back. The hairs on the back of her neck tightened, strained against the flecks of drying blood. It was waiting for something.

Painfully, she got her weight onto her left leg and pushed up. Her wound screamed against the movement, faux bandages forced into it with the unsteady manoeuvre, but she was up and tipping into the movement to let herself bump ass first into the upper ledge, legs snug to the steps as she lumbered herself, ungainly, onto the wood. The blood-thing was wobbling now, the mirror shards swinging closer each time it dipped, and she kept skirting away until her back met the loveseat and she could leverage herself up.

She hitched her arm on the seat, gripping to leverage her weight so she could lean into her right. Her palm, still covered in sweat and painful from digging into the pit edge, slid off the frame and she dropped, the side of the seat skidding up into her armpit as she caught herself on the cushions. It jarred up into her shoulder with the impact. The bounce of the chair off her ribs hurt, pushed the air out of her in shock, and she doubled over into the material with a crunch loud in her ears. She flinched, head ringing from the knock against the wooden leg as she struggled to right herself, everything too blurred, a spinning like her brain was twirling within her skull. She couldn't focus: her vision swam.

The creature was rushing towards her in waves, the sloshing steps pushing through her confusion to grip her heart with a vivid fear. *Move.* She had to move.

Slamming the poker out in front of her, she folded forward, curling over onto her own legs so she could shove a hand under her knees and pull, thighs to her chest. Groaning, she pushed up on her throbbing feet, grabbing the chair arm so she could get upright, weaving as she whimpered against all the pain. Everything *hurt*, pain focused into sharp points pressing in against her feet, biting into her hip, echoing in her skull. She swung blindly with the poker, one hand clutching the red velvet backing so she could retreat.

There was a thick, hollow sound like a stone dropping into water and the poker tugged as she connected with something, briefly, but it continued through with her momentum.

She clung to the seat as she blinked the room back into clarity, the blood creature on her left. It was oozing on one side; the red leaking out like an overflowing sink, and her poker had a thick band of blood over it, but the creature was still shambling towards her. Being seen wasn't stopping it now, the picture of her screaming face rocking past in mirror flashes as it approached.

This close it was rancid as a butcher's shop in the summer—the dank mouldering of dirty spaces. She gagged, throwing one of the loveseat's cushions at it.

The creature backhanded the cushion, expelling a curve of blood over the seat, and Stephanie. It was *hot*: arterial fresh. She threw the second cushion out of spite, a petty wish to make it work harder.

It took a heavy step closer; the shape distending with the effort, and one thick hand plopped onto the seat back as if reaching for her. She stared it down, the length of the sofa between her and it, her feet moving mindlessly to track back. There was no point running to the corridor: all that awaited out there was Thomas and the void. That left the suite: the pit and the bar.

A speck of gold flashed at her from the pit.

"Oh, fuck you."

She twisted, limping against the pain as she ran for the bar. Passing the fireplace, she swatted the burning stack over the floor behind her, the creature surging with a wet crash. The logs and peat tipped across the floor between fireplace and pit, enough to hurt a human foot. It was something.

Even breathing hurt now, her throat tight as she gulped air, plastering herself against the bar. She spun to find the blood creature pouring itself up, out of the pit steps, the stones coated in a red trail. Clots and abandoned shards glittered in the low light of the spilled fire. She had vague, half-memories of bible stories about blood daubed on stone, offerings of life up to God. Sacrifice. She was no one's fucking sacrifice.

The creature was near boiling now, frothing as it flowed from the steps to reform in front of the bar. The teeth were no longer lined up in a faux smile, jumbled instead around an almost circle on the edges of the face-shape, and the mirror eyes remained, gleaming.

"Go away!" It was pointless to scream at it, almost as pointless as running, but she had to. Had to keep pushing against the insanity of it or she would just lie down and cry. It didn't respond other than to surge, the too-thick arms landing on the bar with the thump of meat hitting a slab. She hefted the poker up between them, grasped in both hands like a length of rope.

The creature tipped itself down, pooling to expand over the bar, knocking over the bottle she abandoned earlier. It toppled and smashed into an explosion of dark green fragments, shooting out over the floor.

Stephanie shook her head as the blood gushed over the lip of the bar top, swirling around her feet. She danced back as if scalded, bumping into the counter in a few scant moves. The fluid followed, shooting up between her still outstretched arms so it was pressed against her body, the mirror eyes so close she could just see her own staring back. The teeth studded around the edges, all pointing towards her.

It scooped its arms around her, pulling her towards the tangle of its face, swollen fingers pressing viciously into her ribs. She cried out, yanking the poker closer to hammer at its back, or whatever it had, but the metal just slid through the crimson shape, bouncing uselessly off her own sternum before sinking back in. Dragging it sideways, her hands jarred, the blood thickening around the bar until it wouldn't move.

The sides of the face curled out, stretching as if it was some profane flower opening, those off-white teeth like petal tips. They were inching closer, clambering for her face as she arched herself away, hands off the poker now to claw the reaching shapes. Her palm made contact, knocking the tendrils into each other with a wet slap that splayed them over the mirror eyes. Something sliced through her back as she slapped harder, smashing the shapes together.

She hissed at the shock of cold pain, one of the arms coming back to show those too-long fingers tipped with something pointed. Squinting at it, she could almost place the shape, a familiarity ridiculous in the current circumstances, her brain racing to bring together the sensation and image.

Razor blades now studded each digit, fractured pieces that came out like claws, pointing at her. The same blade she had seen in the mirror—after the steamed message—the one the blond man had used to cut his throat. They were now being used to pick the bloody strands apart, letting the shards of mirror resurface to draw her nearer. There were more teeth, somehow, the whole round of the face now bordered by them as it shot forward.

"It's too late once you're here!" She shouted the words at her reflected eyes, white all the way around. "Find your own way out or join it."

The creature paused, the pressure at her back abating as it pulled away a fraction. She held her breath as it seemed to peer at her, tilting the non-face this way and that. Her pulse was thick in her throat, no room to drag in air. The blood bubbled again, popping as it trembled, the head sucking back in on itself before it surged forward, wet and hot and coating her face.

The shards sliced sharp as the creature swarmed her, her mouth and eyes screwed shut, her nose flooded by the cloying smell of rotten meat. Fighting not to gag or cough she floundered, beating the jagged arms, yanking herself as far away as she could stretch or twist. She couldn't breathe, the teeth starting to pin-prick press against her skin and wriggle in. Her elbow bumped something solid on her right, followed by the rattle of wobbling glass: the bottles from her intended wine binge.

Twisting an arm free from the bleeding embrace, she groped for what she'd knocked, hand slipping around the cold bottle to close her fingers over the neck. There was no cork, just the undisturbed line of glass, slick from blood.

She gripped tight, as if she were drowning, bringing her arm as high as she could before she slammed it down against the tangled shapes of their faces. The alcohol sloshed out from the impact and though the glass didn't shatter, the blood-being raised back. Crashing the bottle into it again, she took a desperate breath as her face came free; the air flooded with the metallic stink of old blood, the alcohol bouncing over her skin. Gin, she had picked up the discarded optic bottle, and it stung fire across her cuts, but the smell was heavenly—potent and botanical.

The monster shook, flinching in on itself where the alcohol hit. She tipped the bottle upside down, swiping her hand under the flow of liquid so she could wipe her eyes clear, burning clarity. The creature changed, dipping down into the space between the bar and counter. Cowering.

Shuddering at the sight, she stuttered out, "I'm sorry." She didn't know if it was her own sentiment or if she was just finishing the message in the mirror.

She grabbed the wine that had been waiting for her, tipping the already open bottle over what had been the head, now just a nub, watching the teeth swirl into the shoulders as it collapsed into itself, the mirror pieces winking light between the bubbles. She seized the other wine bottle when that one finished, and after that ran dry she pulled the vodka down from the optics, pouring it out into the pile of red tissue and clots at her feet.

Teeth dotted the wriggling mess, flecks of glass and metal bound up in the thick ridges of tissue that remained, twitching. Next, she pulled the tequila down and doused those parts too, finishing with one of the remaining wines from the fridge. Smashing the cork off, she tipped the entire bottle over the teeth and razors, not stopping until all the red was running away in streams of bubbles and clear spirit. The fumes made her light-headed, each breath a new, heady selection of poor memories, and the underlying tinge of metal meant her stomach rolled with an unpleasant insistence.

The music swam back into her focus, a mournful piano piece that made her think of lonely nights, the notes pitching and dropping like someone's sobs. When had it changed? Maybe it had been cheerful before this.

Maybe the hotel was mourning another valued staff member she had killed.

Chapter 16

O nce there was nothing left to pour, she let the bottle drop to the floor, uncaring when it smashed. There were pieces of things everywhere, what did more shards of glass matter?

She plucked up her poker, examining it: the metal had decayed where the blood caught it, a dimpling eating over three quarters of the length. Twisting it between her palms, the damage looped the surface—a small indent into the shape, the roughness like a sheath not quite reaching the handle. She hugged it close for a second before she set it on the bar and began picking her way out.

Aiming for the fireplace, she warily stepped through the bloody flood, setting each step down like a bird testing for worms, popping her foot before she settled her weight. She nicked her feet a few times, the sharp bites of glass or metal hidden in bubbles, but she was content to escape the bar without slicing her soles to ribbons.

The red run-off crept around both sides of the bar, flowing over the wooded floor like an old plague warning: the streaks daubed around infected villages. She sucked a deep breath to steady her swimming head before she crossed in front of the bar, stretching one leg over the current to hop across it and stand before the bathroom corridor. The soaked duvet and towels sat waiting for her, still crimson.

It would be easiest to start with the duvet, logically, but the idea of handling that made her gag. The smell of the alcohol mix wafted over her exposed tongue, and she covered her mouth to control a heave. Acid scorched along the length of her gullet, a bright burn that settled somewhere halfway up, glowing against her chest with the intensity of gin.

She missed being drunk, obliterated by adrenaline. The shaking would start soon. That was inevitable with shock. Should she be shocked anymore? The hotel kept finding ways to surprise her. Out on deployment there had been other options—not just alcohol but weed. Even just a good cup of tea. She'd seen plenty of lads go daft trying to deal with things. PTSD could blast through you just as well as the shrapnel.

Taking a few deep breaths through her mouth to settle her stomach, she bent her knees, grabbing the duvet with both hands in one quick move. It was cold and heavy, the thickening blood staining her fingers like cherry juice. A dull laugh bubbled past the burning, spilling out with more bitterness than the vomit.

It took a couple of hefts before she could peel the cover away from the towels underneath, but she got it, sweeping around to face the room. It left trails of red, the flooded corners brushing over the wood in meandering lines out of time with her steps. Kicking with her right foot, she brushed it over the crawling line of fluid, wafting the material to mop it towards the stone steps.

The message from the mirror rang through her mind: the wish to remain out of the pit. Was sending this down into the darkness some betrayal? She didn't know how long the man had been dead in there. Thomas never had given her a straight answer. Her arms sagged as she tried to weigh up the choice: if she was about to commit some awful sin.

The cut on her brow popped open as she frowned, stinging with new blood, and that was enough to spur her on. Even if it was some unfaithfulness to the mirror lines, he had tried to kill her. Drowning in curdled blood was not a good death, if there was such a thing, and she had no wish to be part of his lonely agony.

She stomped more fluid into the duvet before she rolled it into a long tube, tossing that down the steps. It sagged, leaving vivid marks on the stone as it tripped over the edges and settled at an angle on the lip of the pit. The line of fluid followed it, wicked along by the material, which sank, languidly, down into the darkness. The drop was almost slow-motion, like it was being cradled in the descent, though that was just gravity. Inescapable. Much like her shock. She turned away, back to the bar and the red tide of destruction.

She would have to get rid of the teeth. There was no way she could sleep, even drink, knowing they were scattered over the floor. She might cut her feet more. One of them burrowing into her foot would be worse than the squirming face. There had been a man once, long ago, a Viking earl who had cut off the head of his adversary and displayed it on his horse all the way home from battle. The head had bounced during the ride, teeth grazing into the thigh of the victorious leader, and the gangrene had killed him within weeks of his triumph. She would smash the teeth to bits with a bottle if she had to. Powder them to dust.

If the teeth were to go, she should get the other bits too; the would-be eyes and metal claws. The towels would have to do for that, she could use one of the smaller ones to pick pieces up and bundle them into the biggest bath sheet, tie it together like a knapsack of nightmares and toss them away. She would not look down into the pit. The presence heavy at her back, and she knew the eyes would be there, waiting to gloat. No, none of that.

She needed to take care of her wounds. Wipe them down with a bar cloth, at least, clean off any remains of the sad shower man. Once the parts were gone.

She stepped towards the cramped corridor and stood before the mess of towels, warped together. As she lowered shakily onto one knee, a movement caught her eye, the space behind the bar thrumming with little shifting shapes. She held still, forcing herself to breathe through the stuttering in her chest, the thrash of her heart against her ribs.

Leaning towards the wall, so she could rest her weight on it as she turned, she squinted along the length of the floor between bar and counter. The fizz of carbonated bubbles had been replaced by teeming vibrations of discarded pieces jostling together, bumping to an unsteady beat. It was less a pulse than some insane percussion, at odds with whatever was droning through the room—the fear had silenced that now—and they were pulling slowly towards her.

The teeth really were going to get her. She choked against a laugh, the ridiculousness of it almost enough to breach her distress, the row of white, sharp points ambling after her in blind vengeance. She should get away from them, circle around the edge of the room and double back so she could grab the bottle and really go at breaking them. Or scoop them up into one, have them collected and shown off like pretty rocks from a beach. Would they rattle against the glass like a telltale heart? The hotel would probably steal them back, shift them away with one of the curtain swoops.

She needed to move. Again. Waiting for them to get her would only mean a painful end, be it those teeth or the gleaming razors, but she couldn't make her legs work. The muscles jumped and twitched uselessly; no energy left to run. The march of things coming towards her grew, swelled until they were tumbling over each other to crest from behind the bar and into the open room. There was a deep hiss, like stones as the tide washed into shore and dragged itself back out again.

Then it turned, tossing and bouncing across itself to slip past her and towards the pit, following the meandering blood line over the wood. The mirror pieces bobbed, catching the light briefly as they swirled atop the other fighting parts, a flash of a picture reflected to her—blond hair, sad brown eyes, a glint of metal, billowing steam—then they were gone as the mass reached the stone levels and poured over. The sound was something between breaking glass and heavy rain, disappearing down over the pale steps and joining the duvet.

Stephanie stood, wobbling on her unhelpful legs as she crept towards the pit. The conjoined mass was bobbing as if on water, the mix of bone, glass and metal rolling around the lowest level before it all swirled together and vanished down into the darkness, leaving her alone.

CHAPTER 17

T he music switched into something triumphant, a jolly, bouncing tune. The notion of the hotel being happy made her shudder.

The suite felt abandoned—the floor almost clean following the exodus of the shards, just the russet track of the blood creature's last escape. She blinked to herself, slapping her cheeks to refocus, before going closer to the bar to check behind it. There was a red tint, nothing more.

She picked up her poker, rubbing her hand across the damage: it scratched like sandpaper, the peaked metal raising pink lines over her palm. It would hurt if she whacked something with it. If beating them worked. The aching strip across her ribs where she'd hit herself was a dull reminder of that failing.

Thomas would be waiting for her, to reprimand her for killing another member of the hotel.

There were no spirits left to wipe over her new wounds, or stem the pain budding at her every seam. Wine would be fine to drink but the sugar was an enemy in wound, and it would be better to get them clean again, give anything leaking red a chance to rest overnight. The lights had come on, and the fog outside was dim, so it was evening. Probably. She would need to check the cuts on her back; that was a new challenge. So far she'd kept the injuries to the front, but the sticky pain at her ribs reminded her of the razors. She would need a new top too. So much to repair.

A quick breath rattled out of her, bone tired and sick to her stomach. Her head ached, dagger points of pain behind her eyes, sharp enough that she wanted to push the heels of her hands into the sockets and just pop the orbs so she could massage her optic nerves directly. She should ask Thomas for tips. He liked pointed things.

The corridor was almost as red as the suite, the gory paintings glowing in the lamplight. She peered up into the space, hovering at the entrance to the suite: the sooty residue still adorned the ceiling, but nothing was lurking by the door. Just the same tiles and doors as before.

She kept her eyes forward as she went to the doors, a nagging pain sitting low in her gut. It wasn't the sharp insistence of her wound, though that was an awareness of that creeping in. The display table loomed into the edge of her vision, where the porcelain figures should have been. She paused, staring at the smudged roof, almost unwilling to look at the little statue. The *longing*. God, she missed Jenny.

Swallowing against the pain in her throat, she opened her eyes, looking down to the tabletop. Only one figure remained, the kneeling one, the blue face now tinged with red where there could have been a mouth. It held the head of the other between two stubby, outstretched arms, the rusted wash now intense and near dripping from the shiny stump of a neck. She stared at it for a few long beats, her breath harsh, too quick and jagged, her eyes burning. She walked away. There was little point wiping the tears away until she got to the door; more would just come, so she let them.

Once she reached the frosted glass Stephanie set the poker down in the same corner, wiping her face with both hands. It wasn't as if it mattered that she looked a mess, and her shirt was shredded so she would, but she didn't want him to see her looking weak. In pain was one thing, but distress was different. He'd have to carve that out himself: she wouldn't give him any.

Drying her hands on the tatters of her top, she opened the door so it caught on the latch, the crack of light striping her. There was something so ridiculously normal about that, of waiting behind a door to come through, of thresholds having potential.

She pulled the door open, sucking in a breath as she stepped into the hall. The space was bustling, positively joyous, the ghosts scurrying together like school children on a trip, even the mould brightly coloured and fringing around like bunting. Thomas stood in his usual spot, smirking as she took in the scene. He had depleted, his skin papery and flaking, his eyes dark as a millpond, but the smile stretching his lips until they cracked was genuine. Bright.

"You seem chipper," she said. The rumble of the void began, crackling against the walls.

"I'm delighted. You did very well in your handling of Eric." He nodded to her, the dome of his head reflecting light over the patches now missing hair.

"The man in the shower?"

"He's been a thorn in my side for decades. He was a stain on the suite, malingering in there, making people so pitiful. Desperate. The hotel could never quite shift him. Blood magic is an ancient thing, difficult to diffuse."

A startled laugh shook out of her. "Magic?"

Darkness swamped the staircase across from the door, faster than normal, but it stayed there, simply vibrating rather than tearing the steps asunder.

"Yes. The self-sacrifice in the shower was all very stoic, but he wound up trapping himself. Some interaction between the water and blood with the spirit of the hotel, I don't know the practicalities. Then every time he got another to join him it just tightened the links."

Stephanie nodded, hands itching to grab the poker again. "Did he get many?"

"More than I ever desired. It was such a waste of talent to see him enmeshing himself with those the hotel selected."

"Right. Right. So, he wasn't one of your... special colleagues?"

"Oh no. The hotel thought he could be useful at one time, that's why he was in there, but he was a cancerous waste of investment. Too selfish to see the delight in joining us, and too stupid to kill himself in a way that worked. But he persisted, and stole others when they became too maudlin."

Stephanie nodded again, like it was reasonable, like any of it made sense. "He went into the pit. Well, the bits."

"I'm sure the Basker will make use of what's left, though how much sentience there can be in dribs and drabs of desperation I don't know."

He paused, giving a little shrug. "Certainly won't be training him up like we will you."

The comment stung like a slap, one pain a reminder of another. "I need painkillers, or more alcohol. I'm covered in cuts."

He hummed, spurts of dark blood bubbling out of the holes in his chest as he shook his head. "We may have a slight problem there. While I am thoroughly pleased at your handling of Eric, the hotel feels your actions were somewhat...wasteful. The bar will be restricted."

Her eyebrows shot up, the cuts opening again. "Excuse me?"

"I think it's a little harsh, I do, but the Basker has a strict policy in relation to waste."

"There's nothing else to keep my wounds clean."

"Cauterisation is still available, I believe, and you will still have alcohol. It will just be less abundant. Apparently it's common in hotels now."

She gritted her teeth, close to grinding them. "Can I get paracetamol, at least?"

"I'm afraid not."

"Of course not. What's the plan, just make me miserable until I give in?" She crossed her arms over her sore ribs, holding her top close to her skin.

"Perhaps the hotel thinks meeting your needs hasn't given you the necessary incentive."

"Fuck you. Getting me to do your dirty work then rewarding me by taking things away?"

"I had no say in this. I am merely a servant of the Basker."

"Whatever you say." Her breath shook in her chest, vision flashing white as her anger overtook the growling void. "I want to go home. I want to see my partner!"

"You're not leaving. We went over this when you entered the suite."

"There has to be a way."

"Just death, and the lonely embrace of the grave."

"'The grave's a fine and private place, but none, I think, do there embrace'—very Andrew Marvell. Did you like him, before you became this?"

He hummed, mock consideration dripping from him along with the dark blood. "I've always appreciated poetry."

"Does the hotel still let you? How long have you been here?"

"Time becomes immaterial in a role of service."

She hissed air at his deflection, blood at the back of her teeth as she bit into her cheek. "You were a person, once."

"So was Eric, but you killed what he became."

"He would have killed me."

"Certainly. And you will die by other means here. You should make it worth something."

"I hate you, you know?"

"I'm sure we'll have time to work on that once you join us."

"Maybe I'll just jump into the void, cheat you and the damn hotel. If I'm dead either way, I'd prefer oblivion to time spent underneath *you*." She spat blood at him when she turned to go, clipping into the door in her rush. Her side sang in pain.

"One tip, if I may?" She stilled, glancing over her shoulder at him. "Eric was quite the corrosive character. The bitterness got to him. Your little tool might not be as useful anymore."

"I'm not giving it back."

She grabbed the poker as the door shut, holding it up. The damage had eaten deeper into the metal, the peaks now sharper, maybe half a centimetre. Corrosive indeed. She dropped it, kicking back into the door with her left foot as she screamed. It wasn't even words, just a howling wail that had been trapped somewhere between her hammering heart and her fear.

She sank down onto the floor, hand going to the poker, just in case, and cried into her knees. Her throat hurt, and sobbing made it worse, and she couldn't see properly with tears over her lashes. Rocking her head back to rest against the door, she tried to breathe through her running nose before she became a hiccoughing mess.

The hotel wouldn't give her another poker. Or maybe it would, and it would be one of those stupid miniatures you got in the dreadful country sets, as long as a slipper and almost as useless.

She wiped the back of her wrist across her eyes, peering at the metal again. She brought it close, trying to focus on where the damage began, how much she would have left if it continued to decay. After the handle, the metal was normal for about the breadth of her palm, then it sank in, jagged little needle teeth pushing up. There was the lingering odour of blood, a different metallic tone to the cold iron. With any luck that would go away once the damage stopped, or the weakened metal dropped off.

She wouldn't touch that bit again while the reaction was going on. She could work with just the handle, bundle a pillow around it when she went to bed. It might not eat through a whole pillow overnight. She needed to go back to the room and clean herself with whatever this reduced version of the bar was.

She just wanted to lie down.

CHAPTER 18

- -

The art was mercifully static, still bloody spectacles and glowing gore. It was almost a comfort, this blood remaining where it should. She dragged herself closer to the suite, almost passing the little table without thinking. It stood out from the wall a touch, though, and her hand brushed the wood. The figure wobbled, unsteady with the new weight at the arms, and she cocked her head to watch it teeter. The rocking caused an almost clock-like ticking as the base circled the wood, ramping up quicker as it settled. She smashed the poker across it before it could right itself, limping away.

The bar was still there, not missing entirely. Optics stood empty, bare metal without even a measuring cap, and underneath them sat a squat, black fridge. The door was solid, so she couldn't see the contents, but she recognised it from enough years travelling for work: a minibar.

"Quite the cut back." No one was here to hear her. The room was back to meticulous normality—the fire burning, lights mercifully dim. It even made the bed.

Circling around the seat, she revelled in the heat from the flames, stopping beside it to let the backs of her legs warm up. It wasn't that she was cold, exactly; the room was always something like temperate, but the heat was a rare physical comfort to anchor onto. She couldn't burn her anxieties out with spirits anymore.

She stared at the pit as she let her skin tingle, the darkness of it seeming more. Thicker. It wasn't just the lights; they were dimmer than the faux daylight of the windows, but there were no eyes or lips lurking to torment her. A chill breeze rolled up, the hair on her arms rippling into a line of prickling awareness. They looked like the damaged poker pieces, sharp and wary.

This wouldn't get her anywhere. There was a minibar to inspect, and cuts to tend to. And she'd need a new top. The old one could burn, the tickle of cold skimming across her skin through the cuts a reminder of how bare her back and sides were.

She pulled the top off, tossing it into the fire. She had enough spares in her case, and rags at the bar, no point holding onto useless things. The material hit the logs with a heavy sigh, dimming the light behind her enough to make her shadow jump and elongate over the pit. It was a stupid echo of the hotel's desire, not hers, and she turned from it towards the bar.

There were still two stools behind the bar—lonely company together. She pulled one around to sit, perching on it as she set the poker beside her leg and opened the minibar. It was brightly lit inside, little rows of bottles lined up like a graveyard, clear spirits all the way back. They were miniatures, of course, though the solitary wine bottle stood in front of the fruit juices was full sized. Great, she could drink half of that and top it up with the spirits like she was some idiot student at a house party. Or she could clean her wounds and see what she had left afterwards, count the discarded empties like collectors' editions. That would be better.

"I know what you're doing, by the way," she said over her shoulder. The pit didn't respond. She shook her head, setting a finger on the small vodka cap and wobbling it back and forth. Wiping down the wounds was most important. Then she could sleep.

Grabbing two miniatures out, she popped the caps off with a metallic crack, discarding them along the bar. The cloths were refreshed nearby, and she grabbed one, drizzled the first measure out. The cloth drank it up, just a meandering stain to show the result. She folded it in half and wiped it over the wounds in her face. Everywhere the alcohol touched flared in luminous, bitter pain, her jaw tightening against it.

She huffed a breath, shaking her face to dispel the fumes, then dropped the cloth into her lap. Reaching around her torso, she ignored her bra straps to gauge the cuts on her back, and how much spirit they would need. They were in lines all together, three or four to a group, and her skin was sticky with dried blood. Hers, at least. Luck was with her enough that they were shallow: there was no gaping like her hip. It would hurt to sleep on them, but she would be safe.

Grabbing the cloth again, she flipped the second bottle over, wrapping it in the cloth to form a makeshift drip feed, alcohol glugging out as little bubbles filtered up the neck. The pain was still there but less toothy, pushed away from her by the focus on not wasting the vodka while she wiped. Sharp flares hissed when the scabs broke away with her motion, fresh blood hot over her skin. It would all dry down, the alcohol would evaporate in her body heat, and sleeping would be easier once she had a top on too.

Her hip wound was throbbing, made worse by her squirming on the stool to get both sides of her back. She set the empty miniatures against the back of the bar, as far from the edge as she could. There had been enough shattered glass on the floor tonight.

Drumming her hands on the fridge door, she looked at the blank, black surface, and how the light played over the paint. Her silhouette blocked some, darkness defined by how closely she leaned in to look, and the warm shine over the door was a welcome reflection, the suite in negative. She watched it move with her as she swayed this way and that, smirking to herself at the silliness: she hadn't even started on the gin yet.

Just as she swung back so she could get the wine, the light dipped, a thick line of darkness spreading out from each side of her shadow head. She stilled, swiping a hand around her hair to see if anything was sticking up. The dark lines remained, growing thicker as she heard ragged, wet breathing behind her.

She spun on the stool to face the room. There was nothing—no one—just herself and the crackle of the fire. Her top was flaming, the edges curling over the peat stack as it burned up. There was nowhere for something to hide, the pit leaving nowhere to hide. She glanced back to the minibar, only her own shadow there. She grabbed the door, scooping the wine out and plucking the poker up by the handle. Bed it was.

Dropping the bottle into the middle of the covers and setting the poker next to it, she pulled her case free, the lid still undone despite it being shoved away in the suite reset, and pulled out her remaining travel top. It was longer sleeved, loose, but it would do to sleep in. She could pick something else tomorrow.

A scratch of metal on stone tore through the room and she turned on her heel, pushing herself back into the wall. Nothing moved, the air as still as the breath she held, and after a few silent seconds she let it out in a slow exhale. Maybe it had been the stool.

She flipped the lid closed, kicking the case away so she could lower herself onto the bed and grab the bottle. Fiddling with the metal wrap, she tore into it after a few fumbles, her fingers slick with sweat, and popped the cork with a shudder. It wasn't like a gunshot, she knew them, could sleep through them in the right places, but it boomed through the room and sent her shoulders up around her ears. She went to put the bottle to her lips, tasted the glass, but stopped.

No. Fuck it.

If it was playing stupid with her, she might need the wine for later. She sagged back against the pillows, huffing air. She hadn't even looked for a wine glass, too unsettled, and she didn't know if she could take finding them miniaturized as well, tea party portions.

We're all mad here, went the quote, but she wasn't going to be joining that Cheshire fucking smile in the pit.

She set the bottle down on the floor beside the bed. She could throw it away tomorrow, if it was flat, or it would be gone when she woke up and a new one in the fridge.

The poker was the next problem, those sharp points growing. They would scratch her up in the night, as sure as anything else in this hungry room, but she didn't trust not having it. She settled on sacrificing one of the pillows, tucking it lengthways around the metal so the handle and tip stuck out at opposite ends. It was makeshift, but the pillow was squishy enough to stay in place around the poker. It should last the night, if the corrosion didn't eat through it before then.

She set her fingertips on the bindings on her hip, tapping against the crest of the bone under the skin and material. It hurt, but no worse than it had before Eric, and she wouldn't meet trouble halfway. There was no itch or pinch of infection. She let the bindings be.

She shuffled around, worming her way under the covers and pulling the pillow-poker in too. It settled into the emptiness beside her, a misshapen impression of a body sharing the bed. Stephanie turned her back on it, keeping one hand back to rest on the handle. The stretch of her arm was a low tug at her shoulder, but she could settle into it, digging herself deeper into the covers.

The bed dipped with the weight of something pressing down on her ankle, the grip as gentle as a cat's paw despite the bone-deep pressure. The wet breathing was back, laboured. Darkness from the covers swamped her, vexing as she struggled free from the hot little cave she had made to sit up, blinking, in the low light. The weight at her ankle vanished as she moved, the breathing sucking away into a buzzing silence that made her ears prickle and pop like she'd shifted altitudes.

Golden eyes were at the end of the bed, shiny as new pennies and gleaming with rapacious hunger. The smile was full of teeth, just as golden as the lips, and sharp little claws sat at the end of the covers, pinpoint indents studding the material. There was still nothing else there, no body, no shape bar the bare impression of a face, and it was leering at her, swaying at the edge of the duvet like it wanted to creep closer.

"Oh, get to fuck!" She grabbed for the wine bottle blindly and flung it overhand as soon as she got a hold of the glass neck. It arced towards the non-face, an inevitability to the angle of descent, even as fluid spilled out, sure to go into the eyes. The row of claws shot out and knocked it away, the bottle sailing off towards the corridor, smashing. Stephanie didn't dare look to see what it hit. The face grinned wider, all those sparkly teeth on show, before it blinked slowly at her and retreated. She watched it go, sitting higher in the bed to see it wisp back over the stone, sinking out of view when it dropped under the lip. She sobbed, grabbing her throat to choke the sound, eyes burning as she stared at where it had been.

CHAPTER 19

The cold woke her, shivering and stiff. She'd bundled into the covers again, once the fear had abated and tiredness washed over her in a remorseless tide, the poker-pillow cuddled to her chest as a pitiful security blanket. Those covers had shifted in the night, bundled at her feet in a messy line that had almost tipped from the bed. She still held the poker, at least.

She curled into herself, muscles screaming in protest as she flexed and stretched, checking them over limb by limb. Everything moved as it should, tight but otherwise operative, and she ghosted a hand over her hip to check for any damage in the night. It hurt, but there was no additional heat, and her leggings were clean, so she slowly sat up.

Her top stuck in a few spots, tugging against her skin, but she peeled it free in a careful line, reaching both hands around and pulling the material away. Some scabs popped, blood swelling, but she could move smoothly as she leaned this way and that, the fluid smearing. She forced her shoulders down, rubbing her arms with the opposite hands to warm the complaining muscles.

It was darker than usual and she squinted around, looking at the fire. It was dull and cold, the peat and wood burned down to ashes. The lamps were off, and nothing gleamed in the dark, the room still and black as the pit. She had the impulse to shake the covers out, make sure the eyes and mouth weren't waiting underneath to lure her into sleeping. Not that she would. She was too awake to try lying down again, and she didn't want to tax her wounds.

The air was frigid, the coldest she had been, and she shivered against it as she inspected the room. The windows were gone, sandstone brick where the fog should be, wet by the glint of what little light she had. Burnished gold, a candleflame behind frosted glass, something that let the oozing show.

She swallowed, felt the tang of blood on the back of her tongue. Setting the poker-pillow behind her, she shuffled up onto her knees, peering around for whatever else was here. She was not going to inspect the bleeding wall. No. Fuck that. She hadn't survived deployment and PTSD and nightmares and this *fucking room* to walk into that much of a trap.

"Fuck you," she said, sinking back into sitting.

A roaring screech echoed out of the pit, followed by a crashing bellow. It was like a river had spouted in the centre of the room, the gushing air wet and stagnant, a thundering that shook the bed. A crash signalled the minibar had fallen, the crisp crunch of broken glass mingling with the cracking stone, and the fire set spilled across the floor with the grace of a discarded wind chime.

A choking darkness swamped over the room, as thick as the velvet curtains, pluming out of the pit to flood the stone steps and careen towards the bed. She fumbled for the poker, yanking against the half-destroyed pillow, before a moist slap echoed up towards her. Her arm froze, the slithering grind of something heavy being dragged over stone fixing her to the bed.

The face swooped towards her, eyes and smile wild, the claws gleaming as they sank in above her collarbone and tipped her back onto the mattress, poker jammed underneath her. She screamed into the face, mirroring its gaping mouth, the hungry eyes savouring her. This close she could see they weren't just claws but hands—tiny and thin as bone, the paper-skin like Thomas's—with an iron grip as they wormed into the thick muscle at her shoulders.

Behind the smiling mouth was a gelatinous head, round as a lollipop, translucent and shimmering, which ran into a tubular neck. That vanished into a long, writhing body as thick as the pit. It was scaled, the colour of sea-worn glass and rotting vegetation, and pulses rippled along the dense muscle like a heartbeat. The eyes rolled away from her as the head tipped up, the arms lengthening as a row of spindly, sharp teeth as long as butchers' knives crested out and the jaws—hidden, until now, in the body—pushed forward.

The claws drew her towards the teeth, twisting within her, and she screamed, her pinned arm clutching for the poker handle pressed into her shoulder. Her palm wrapped around it and she pitched herself forward, bashing against those dark, dripping teeth, forehead springing with blood as they crunched together, before the metal slid free of her bodyweight. The biting claws dragged her, raising her from the bed, but she swiped the poker into the gangly arms, grinning at metal tearing through them and the crackling snap, like kindling being split as a fire took hold.

The face jerked back down, teeth retreating and the heavy body slapping onto the bed, dragging her with it. She kept swinging, shoving her left hand under herself to keep upright as she bounced against the mattress, legs knocked open by the crushing weight of the creature on her lower body. She hammered the poker into the drooping head like she could burst it open: hacking strikes that made it loll back and forth. The stumps of the severed arms flailed at her, whacking against the hands embedded in her skin, the golden eyes stricken. She gripped the poker in both hands, ignoring the bursting pinch at her left hip so she could beat the bar into the head, the jaws, the glimmering scales.

The poker snapped: the corroded metal flying away from her to tumble over the edge of the bed. She held the jagged, remaining end up, her knuckles white, both arms shaking as the creature twitched and hissed. The pulpy face loomed closer, gold lips opening to spill black, shimmering ooze, and as it lurched forward she fumbled with her grip. Twisting the handle around so she could swipe it down, she clutched tightly with both hands and stabbed with the little strip of metal she had left. She shoved it into the swollen head until it pierced through the thick skin, more black blood spilling out, pounding the poker tip into the mattress underneath.

Yanking the metal free, she plunged it in again, and again, screeching as she stabbed, the thin neck jerking at each hit like it was electrified, the large body shivering with displeasure. She kicked at the snake-like muscle pinning her, her right heel thumping uselessly into the wall of flesh, the unfathomable cold leeching into her leg. The creature shifted, a dragging noise like sand being sliced erupting as it slipped from the bed and back towards the pit.

The body picked up speed as it retreated, coils whipping away as it disappeared down the hole and the long line of muscle followed. It pulled the ruined head along in the wake and Stephanie gripped onto the poker handle tighter, crying out as she was dragged along the mattress and ruined covers until she nearly pitched off the frame, finally relinquishing her weapon.

She held her breath as the rotten-green scales vanished, the air in the room rushing after it. Her lungs burned as she listened, perched like a gargoyle, too afraid to close her eyes. Other than her frantic blood she couldn't hear anything.

Flashes of the creature pushed at her between one blink and the next: the impossible thickness of the body, the arctic chill against her skin. The spiteful eyes.

Sinking hard on the mattress she heaved a gulp of cold air, jittery as adrenaline settled and pain pushed up in its place. Dark goo rested across her thighs and arms, cold enough to burn, and her palms were bloody with torn blisters. She slapped her legs, the flaring heat in her left hip reasserting itself, and pushed herself into standing.

The room rocked with a vicious lurch. She was thrown back on the bed, flinging herself to one side so she bounced onto the floor instead, grunting as she hit the wood. The claws, still embedded in her skin, jarred into her shoulders, frail, severed hands crunching and ripping free as her own crashed out to break her fall. Her hip was an all-consuming, white void over her vision—devastatingly sharp—and she slammed her fist into the floor to refocus, shoving her hips back so she could scrabble up. Her bloody palms left smearing trails as she struggled for grip.

The suite was shaking, tugging each way as the rumble from the pit became the hiss of glacial melt, the promise of an immense weight about to crash. She turned, ran, limping, into the corridor, tipping into the corner when the room rolled under her feet.

The wall was unyielding, bruising as she landed on her forearms. She shoved off, crashing into the opposite side and knocking the paintings from the walls, heavy frames tilting towards her as she rattled onwards. She surged, feet clumsy but moving, bumping along the wall as she aimed for the frosted doors.

The display table clipped her hip, and she saw the statuette was back, the kneeling figure now cloaked in red, the severed head cracked clean in two. She grabbed it, a stupid impulse, her hand missing the weight of the poker. Crushing it to her chest with one hand, the other guided her along the wall, slapped away portraits as they threatened to tip into her path, her vision blurred like she was lost in smoke.

The doors were close; she could see the fuzzed reflection of her stumbling nearer, then the corridor flooded black as the lights winked out. She lunged forward, lurching against the wall to find the buttons. The metal flayed across her skin, shearing her palms open, but the pustulous bumps slid under her fingers as a wet dragging entered the far end of the corridor. She jammed the buttons randomly, hopelessly trying to force the room to change so the creature would be mangled in it – or at least slowed down - gritting her teeth as the passage shook harder. Her right hand landed on the door handle, and she wrenched it open.

Her feet caught on something as she surged out, slamming the door behind her before she righted herself against the frame. Red smeared across the metal and glass as she checked the handle again, shaking it towards her to make sure it was closed.

The crisp sound of smashing reached her before the pain of the impact, her head strobing with the distanced, spinning ache. She twisted on her feet, tipping into the door, as Thomas's hands dropped the remains of what he'd hit her with and sank into her throat.

"You're not going anywhere!" His face was a withered snarl, the tissue-skin stretched taut over his skull in a grimace. She gulped for air, his fingers squeezing tighter as she fumbled for purchase on the door, the vibrations from within getting stronger. Smashing the statue she still clutched into his temple was less skill than flailing desperation, lashing out to get him away, and he reeled back towards his tiled circle.

"What is that thing?" She darted from the door into the hall, halfway towards the staircase she had watched disintegrate so many times. The entire space seeming to shiver and breath with a clinging, green mould that draped from the ceiling and walls, limp tendrils hanging down like seaweed. Brushing her skin.

"All you had to do was join us, be something more than yourself. Are you so blind that you can't see its majesty?" He seethed as he spoke, his shrivelled eyes gleaming.

"What I saw was—I don't even know."

"Exquisite."

She shook her head. "Vicious, and not something I want to be part of!"

"Then there's no use for you."

He advanced on her again, hands going for her neck, aiming to back her up to the wall, the embrace of the wet strands. *Absolutely fucking not.*

She barrelled into him instead, sending them both onto the dirty floor. A dull roar kicked through the room, distant thunder that bounded off the walls too much for Stephanie to tell if it was the creature or the void. She didn't care. He wheezed as she landed on top of him, a fetid breath puffing up into her face, then he shoved her jaw so her head knocked back and blood flooded her eyes.

Stephanie gagged, coughing against the dry coating in her throat, battering her hands into his chest and neck to scratch for purchase. Heaving her hips up she straddled him, weaving back as he swiped at her eyes, grabbing her hair to yank sideways.

She dipped with his pull, a sickening, loose feeling slipping under part of her scalp, blood spitting over her ear, but she bore her fingers into the holes in his chest, curling them into gnarled hooks to pull him up then crash back down. Black ooze sprayed over the tiles as she smashed him against the floor, and he started to laugh, a clicking, brittle sound as she slammed him down again.

"Don't tell me you're *happy* about this." She wiped at her eyes, clearing the film of russet burning into her.

He was grinning like the pit face, with a hungry certainty. "No, it's quite agonising, but the Basker is coming for you. There's nowhere for you to run."

The door shook, a crack threading out from the stone above the threshold. It wobbled for a tremulous beat, then the ceiling split, showering them in a deluge of stinking water. Thomas laughed harder, head rocking she stared at him.

"I'm not dying here."

"Your precious little stick's gone. You've nothing left to fight with," he spat, the words burbling from his choked mouth.

"You're right." She grabbed his skull, skin splitting in her grasp, and slammed his head down once, twice, a third time to be sure. The bone crunched like a dry leaf and his face tore in two, hissing spores into the air. She spat at the skull as she struggled to stand.

Her hip was freely bleeding, the slash of agony pushing forward with each breath, and the door bucked as something battered against it. She turned to the shaking wood, glancing around the hall. Tiles buckled and twisted, the walls rippled with rot like a bristling cat, and the busy ghosts were gone.

Just her and the Basker.

Claws emerged at the bottom of the door - longer than before, sleek and midnight dark—splintering the edges, and she twisted on her heel to run towards the staircase.

The flat blackness of the void was partway down the stairs, their frayed layers shifting as if caught in a breeze, and she grit her teeth when she reached the bottom step. She closed her eyes, blocking out the pain and the crunching of shattering wood, the stench of rot and corruption. Instead, she thought of Jenny: their warm home, the cats, their stupid Sunday morning rituals.

She would take her chances with the void if her last thoughts could be Jenny. Could be home.

The ragged breathing was behind her again when she dived up the dissolving stairs, pitching into the blackness.

Chapter 20

For a ludicrous moment, she thought she was at a fair. Her stomach flipped, vomit trickling up her throat to swell out in a pathetic dribble, and a wall of dissonant sound swamped over her as multicoloured lights bled together.

She was spinning, tossed around like she had tripped into the ocean, slices of vision flicking over her: the pit, the Basker, the puff of air when Thomas's face split in two.

Her knees met tarmac with a gritty crunch, hands landing in front to catch herself before her face made the same sound. Her palms screamed, the wet road eating into raw flesh anew, and rain was gently soaking her. It was tarmac, a road, the black, coarse material digging into her exposed muscle. She shivered, almost dropping onto her elbows, jitters shaking down her limbs.

A blaring horn sounded to her right and she jolted, flinching sideways. A large form was bearing down on her, growling as it approached, luminous white eyes round as saucers, a tall grill of silver teeth bared in a grimace.

Something in her leg snapped, clean as a twig under a foot, and then she was sinking into the blackness below.

There were things stuck in her. Rigid shapes under her skin—at her hands and the soft space at the crook of her elbow—pieces that tugged as she shifted under the weight draped across her.

"Stephanie?" Jenny. Her eyes struggled open, seeking the voice to see if she was real. Jenny was in a chair beside her, face much too thin, her hair straggly and heavy with grease. She'd been crying; her eyes were redder than when she tried to do eyeliner without a stencil.

"Baby?" Her voice creaked like an old door, misshapen in her throat.

"Here, drink something." Jenny pressed a bottle to her lips, tipping it up in little dips so she could take in swigs. Stephanie let the water sit on her tongue for a few seconds, her whole mouth tacky. Everything was fuzzy: the covers she was under, the gown with a split down the side she was bundled in, too big for her by far, the wraps around her head that pushed into her left eye's field of vision.

Buzzing strip lights glared above her and a pair of tall, thin windows with the grid-pattern lace of protective glass showed a darkened view of a city. Towers topped with blinking red lights and lines of glowing windows stood back in the distance, a carpet of lights smattered across the houses that sat closer. A lamp leaned over the bed she was in, a spotlight on her aching face, and a cluster of luminous machines flanked around her head. Jenny sat on one of two synthetic chairs that looked like they should have been in a school assembly hall, half shaped and wonky legged, on the shiny, plastic tile floor.

"Where are we?" Stephanie asked.

"Glasgow, in hospital. You were in an accident."

"I remember a road." There had been rain, a horn. She'd been on hands and knees, rippling with pain.

"A taxi hit you. It broke your leg and, did some other damage. You were lucky it was one of the speed-controlled lanes. Turns out Glasgow has lots of them."

"I don't remember it."

"They said you might not. Or just bits, flashes of it. Before that..." She paused, looking at the half-open door. Shuffling the chair closer with an ungainly shriek of plastic against plastic, she took Stephanie's bandaged right hand, lacing their fingers together and squeezing. The blue veins under Stephanie's intact skin were vivid, more prominent under the lights. "I'll have to go and tell them you're awake. They said I shouldn't mention anything until you brought it up, but, I just want to say that it's okay. Whatever's happened, I'm still with you. Team us, yeah?"

"Like if I can't walk? Was the break that bad?"

"Not that, but yeah, it was." She looked down at their hands, sighing around her bitten lip.

"Tell me."

"You were gone weeks, Stephy. I know you wouldn't have left me like that, even after that stupid row, and the wounds weren't just from the taxi. Some of them are older. Severe."

A shimmer of understanding loomed in her mind, gossamer and gold. "I don't remember."

"That's okay. You don't have to right now, maybe you don't have to ever. Whatever works for you. They're going to want to get the police in, at some point, and we're going to get you good counselling when you're ready for it, just like we did before. Yeah?" Jenny looked up at her, lashes glittering, and gave her hand a little squeeze of reassurance.

Stephanie couldn't speak, her throat closed by the memory of rotten water, coiling blood. She nodded, pressing their fingers tighter together. Jenny's smile was crumpled, and tear stained, but true. Just as bright as Stephanie remembered. "Okay. But I want to go home."

"Soon as we can, we will. Chris'll be fed up with the cats by now anyway." Jenny wiped at her eyes, letting go of Stephanie's hand. "I'll go get the nurse, stay here."

"Thought I might go shopping first." Tears spilled down her aching cheeks at the dumb joke, afraid to let their fingers separate.

"I'll be right back, promise." She pecked a kiss to Stephanie's forehead—dipping closer to press their chest together in a semblance of a hug—then slipped out the door.

Stephanie leaned back in the bed and closed her eyes, breath shaky as she sucked in the too-clean air, antiseptic clinging to her nostrils. Her stomach was a hollow itch, too demanding to settle. The backs of her eyelids teemed with shapes: golden lips, flaming antlers, the staring eyes of so many paintings. Opening them again, she checked the room for lurking faces.

Her left hand had the least things attached to it, still covered in dressings but mostly free, and she shoved it under the white woollen blanket, tugging the side of her robe open. Her left hip was bound up, bandages stretching over plain white underwear in a much neater loop than she had managed. Her hip bones pressed up at the edge of her skin like teeth, a perilous dip showing the concave of her stomach. She'd never been this thin, she was always solid with muscle underneath a softer layer. Her wrists were so bony, the tendons at the back of her hands a rigid fan amongst the blue veins.

She reset the material, smoothing the cover down, propping her chin in her right hand palm as she rested the elbow on the safer hipbone.

"I got out." She tapped two fingers on her lips, glancing around the room. She couldn't run with a broken leg, and the soft distance from the rest of her body signalled she was sedated, so she'd be limited in what she could do.

"Quite the trick." A woman stood in the doorway, short red hair glowing in the bright lights. A large bouquet filled her hands.

Stephanie swallowed, a shout dying in her throat. "Frankie."

"Pleased you remember me." Frankie stepped into the room, bringing a waft of sweet rot and pollen with her. She was dressed nicer than in the bar, a pair of neat black slacks and a silky white blouse. A small waistcoat still nipped her waist in, now dark purple tartan with green accents that sang against her hair and freckles.

"You're looking good for a ghost."

"I've had a promotion. Since Thomas...left us, a new concierge was needed, and I've been with the hotel a long while."

"How are you outside?"

"I'm new in my role; I get more leeway before I settle in. And I will settle in. I'm so good with people." She flashed Stephanie a wide smile, tipping her chin up to show a vicious slice down one side of her neck. That had been her exit from the room, then.

Stephanie shivered in her sheets, giving a small nod. "What do you want?"

Frankie came closer, the huge bunch of flowers set on a small cabinet beside the bed. They were nice, flashes of golden accented fascinators threaded between the roses and carnations. Small bodies dropped from the foliage, maggots wriggling around on the pristine white wood. "I wanted to see what you'd managed to get out with. Most of us only bear the final scar; you seem to have collected a few."

"I was enthusiastic."

Frankie grinned, a thin trickle of red running down her incisors. "So you were. Poor Thomas, he didn't know what hit him. Too comfortable in his job." She tapped her fingernails against the cast over Stephanie's leg, the clicking loud in the small room.

"Jenny will be back soon. With nurses."

"Well, I'll not keep you. I just came to see the stalwart victor. Not many like you. Any, in fact." Her grip tightened on the cast and Stephanie bit into her lip, tensing for more pain. Maybe the drugs would help.

"I'm not exactly pretty just now."

Frankie laughed, patting the cast with enough force that a wave of nausea rippled up Stephanie's abdomen. "You're much too harsh on yourself, hen; you've done well. I'm thrilled for you, honestly. I'd still be behind the bar if you hadn't torn Thomas apart like that." She stepped back, turned towards the door before she looked back over her shoulder. "Oh, I did want to say: as long as I'm concierge there's always a room for you, at the Basker."

"You think I'd want to go back?"

"I'm told the dreams become quite terrible. Guilt, fear, flashbacks."

"How would you know that if no one else got out?"

Frankie shrugged, hands falling at her hips. "It's from the suicides. You remember Eric? Lots of wailing and weeping. At least it'll be quieter with him gone, too."

"Thanks for the tip." Stephanie shifted in the bed, hands inching towards the call button.

"No need for that, petal. I'll be gone in a flash. Just remember; we'll all be waiting for you. The Basker never forgets a guest."

She came back towards Stephanie, leaning in to plant a hot kiss on her cheek. This close Stephanie retched at the smell, so much worse in the antiseptic cleanness of the hospital. It was decay and stagnant water, the smell cloying in her throat and making her stomach twist into action. Frankie laughed, grabbing the cardboard semicircle that was beside the flowers and thrusting it into Stephanie's hands. A smattering of maggots wriggled within but that didn't stop Stephanie throwing up into it, her eyes stinging at the acid rolling up her throat.

"Poor thing. See you soon." Frankie gave a little wave as she walked out, closing the door with a firm click as Stephanie continued to heave. She fumbled for the call button, falling back against the pillows when Jenny and a nurse came into the room before she could push it.

"Stephy, what's happened?" Jenny rushed beside her, the nurse neatly slipping between them to get a fresh vomiting bowl.

"No wonder she's heaving, who left these here?" The nurse tutted, scooping the flowers off the cabinet. They were wizened, desiccated petals scattering along with bugs that fell from the movement.

"Those weren't there before," Jenny said.

"You were probably too worried to spot them. We'll be back in a minute to clean you up, Stephanie, you just stay put." The nurse bustled out and Stephanie glared after her, leaning forward to cough out the last of her stomach contents.

"As if you'd be off anywhere." Jenny rubbed her back, stamping on the bugs as they wriggled on the floor. "They weren't there before; I've counted every damn tile in the room."

Stephanie nodded, wiping her mouth. "I know, baby. We should head home."

"We will. We can even stop over somewhere like the Lake District if you want to, not tire you out too much in the one trip?"

"No. Straight home." Stephanie's eyes burned again, the flash of Frankie's bloody smile, and neck. "I want to see the cats."

Jenny's smile didn't reach her eyes but she nodded, patting Stephanie's hair. "Yeah, course. We'll go as soon as we can."

ABOUT THE AUTHOR

Charlotte Platt

Charlotte Platt is a horror and dark fantasy writer based in the very far north of Scotland. When she isn't telling dark tales she can be found walking around rivers and coastal paths with their very anxious collie dog, Joe, or listening to podcasts. She is also a part-time carer for her parents.

ACKNOWLEDGEMENTS

....

Thank you to Rebecca Cuthbert for being the most enthusiastic editor I've worked with, to the Undertaker Books team for making this book so easy to play with, and to Sharon for her patience when listening to my nightmares.

Also From Undertaker Books

Ink Vine
Elizabeth Broadbent

Shadows of Appalachia
D.L. Winchester

The Taste of Women
Cyan LeBlanc

Mastering The Art of Female Cookery
Cyan LeBlanc

In Memory of Exoskeltons
Rebecca Cuthbert

Stories To Take To Your Grave: Vol. 1(Anthology)

A Terrible Place and Other Flashes of Darkness
D.L. Winchester

The Triangle + The Deep Double Feature
Robert P. Ottone

Silent Mine

C.M. Saunders

Odd Jobs: Six Files from the Department of Inhuman Resources(Anthology)

Judicial Homicide (Anthology)

Bodily Harm
Deborah Sheldon

The Screaming House
D.L. Winchester

Wilder Creatures
Nadia Steven Rysing

Ninety-Eight Sabers
Elizabeth Broadbent

SELF-MADE MONSTERS
Rebecca Cuthbert

UNDERTAKER BOOKS

www.undertakerbooks.com

If you are a fan of horror stories and tales,
you'll want to follow Undertaker Books.
We're bringing you stories to take to your grave.

SIGN UP FOR OUR NEWSLETTER ONLINE